SPREAD™
VOL. 3: NO SAFE PLACE

SPREAD VOL. 3: NO SAFE PLACE. FIRST PRINTING. DECEMBER 201
ISBN# 978-1-63215-907-6

Published by Image Comics, Inc. Office of publication: 20
Center Street, 6th Floor, Berkeley, CA 94704. **PRINTED IN THE U.S.A. For information regarding the CPSIA this printed material call: 203-595-3636 and provide reference RICH – 714938.**

For international rights, contact:
foreignlicensing@imagecomics.com

CO-CREATED BY
JUSTIN JORDAN and KYLE STRAHM

WRITTEN BY
JUSTIN JORDAN

ISSUE #12 ART BY
JEN HICKMAN

ISSUE #13 ART BY
FELIPE SOBREIRO

ISSUE #14-17 ART BY
JOHN BIVENS

COLORS BY
FELIPE SOBREIRO

LETTERS BY
CRANK!

EDITED BY
SEBASTIAN GIRNER

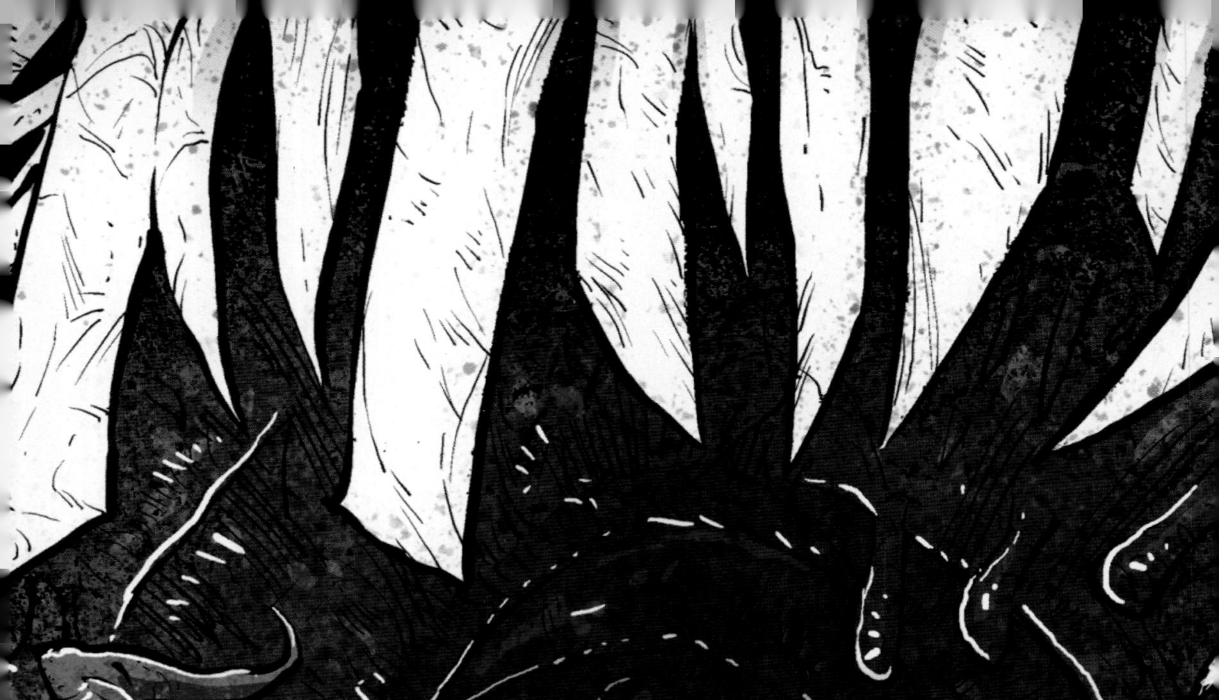

FOREWORD

Once More Into The Breach

Well, we're really cooking now. We've got the secret origin of Molly, courtesy of artist Jen Hickman. We've got the secret origin of Jack, drawn by our very own Felipe Sobreiro. And we've got a glimpse into a side of the Spread we haven't yet seen.

This is roughly the halfway point of our story, and man, I am glad we've made it. Doing a book like this isn't quite as difficult as getting a baby out of the Quarantine Zone, but it's not easy. Seventeen issues so far, and we wouldn't have been able to do it without the support of people like you. So thanks, and I hope you enjoy the rest of the ride.

John Bivens, my old-time buddy and artist on the Image series *Dark Engine* has joined us for this arc. He's a pretty dang good match for the book, and we're lucky to have him on. Kyle is planning on being back down the road, so no worries there.

-Justin Jordan

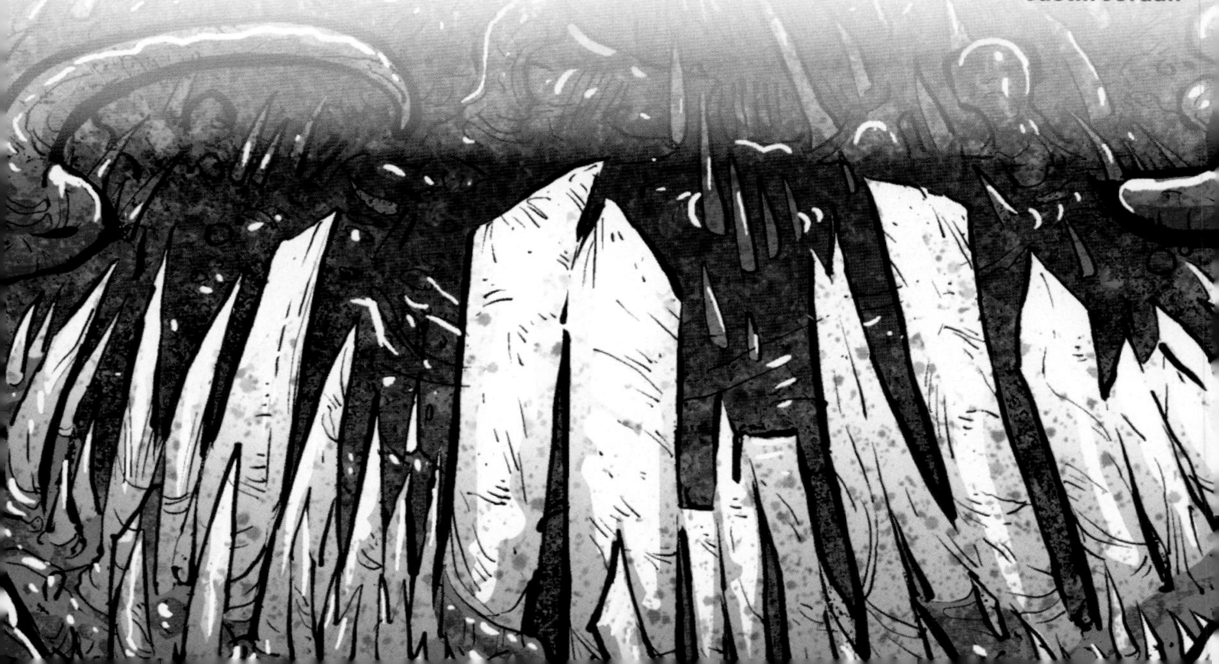

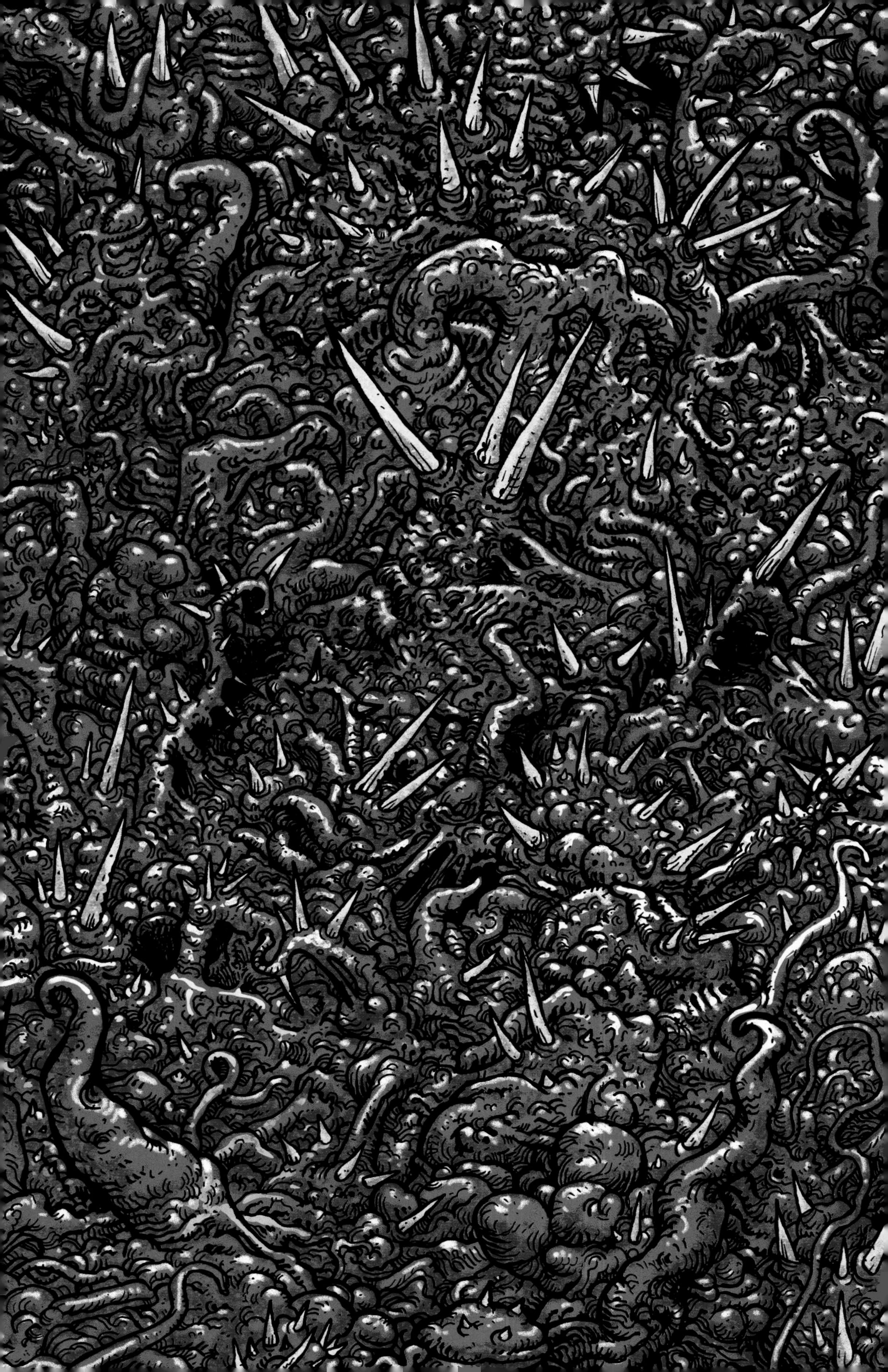

CHAPTER ONE

HI.
NNNNN...
HEY, HEY, IT'S OKAY.
NO ONE IS GOING TO HURT YOU.

RAVEN, I DON'T THINK THAT'S NECESSARY.
I DO.
RAVEN, PLEASE.
...
MY NAME IS JOHN, WHAT'S YOURS?
I KNOW, IT'S SCARY OUT HERE. WHAT'S YOUR NAME?
NNN...
MOLLY.
IT'S NICE TO MEET YOU, MOLLY.
WE CAN'T DO THIS. WE WON'T DO THIS.
WE'RE BARELY SURVIVING, JUST US.
IF WE DON'T DO THIS, THEN MAYBE WE DON'T DESERVE TO SURVIVE ANYWAY.

WELL, IF YOU WANT TO GO UP INTO THE SPREAD AND GET IT FOR YOURSELF, I WON'T STOP YOU.
I DON'T EVEN KNOW IF THIS STUFF IS ANY GOOD.
NOT MY PROBLEM. YOU EITHER WANT IT OR YOU DON'T.
YOU EITHER PAY OR YOU DON'T.
FINE. THESE BETTER WORK OR I'M--
FINISH THAT SENTENCE AND WE'LL FIND OUT IF THESE WORK.
SALVAGER BITCH.
YOU KNOW...
...I CAN FEEL YOU SMILING AT ME.
WELL, ENJOY IT. I DON'T GET MUCH CALL FOR IT.
OH, COME ON, THAT WAS GOOD. "WE'LL FIND OUT IF THESE WORK"?

IT MIGHT HAVE BEEN GOOD HAGGLING.
MAYBE. POSSIBLY.
MIGHT HAVE BEEN?
JOHN MIGHT HAVE TAUGHT YOU TO SURVIVE IN THE DEEP DARK WOODS, BUT I DEFINITELY TAUGHT YOU THAT.
YOU DONE?
WHAT'S WRONG?
RAIDERS. THEY'VE BEEN HITTING HERE AND THEN RUNNING BACK INTO THE SPREAD.
WHY?
SPREAD IMMUNE. HAS TO BE.
THEY STEAL HERE AND GO WHERE PEOPLE CAN'T FOLLOW.
WE COULD FOLLOW.
YEAH, WE COULD, BUT I HAVEN'T KEPT ALIVE THIS LONG TO DIE LIKE...

...THIS--
SHUNK
NO.
NO NONO NO.
HURK...

MOLLY, WE NEED TO GO.
WE CAN'T LEAVE HIM.
I'M SORRY.
WELL, WELL, WELL, AREN'T YOU A PRETTY LITTLE THING?
YES...

...BUT SHE ISN'T *YOUR* PRETTY LITTLE THING.
FINDERS KEEPERS, RACHEL.
I--
SHE'S *NOT* YOURS. AND SHE'S NOT MINE. SHE IS *RAVELLO'S*.
AND IF YOU DON'T LIKE IT, WELL, I CAN END THIS ARGUMENT RIGHT NOW, CAN'T I?
DECISIONS, DECISIONS.
ALL RIGHT, ALL RIGHT.

CHRIST.
IT'S OKAY.
OKAY?
JUST LET ME LOOK AT YOU.
YOU KILLED HIM.
WE DID. AND I'M SORRY FOR THAT.
BUT YOU'RE ALIVE.
BUT I THINK YOU CAN DO BETTER THAN THAT.
DO YOU WANT TO DO BETTER THAN THAT?

YOU'RE SCARED.
GOOD. WE'RE SCARY PEOPLE.
BUT YOU'RE SAFE. NOBODY IS GOING TO FUCK WITH YOU UNLESS THEY WANT TO FUCK WITH ME.
AND THEY DON'T.
COME ON. THERE'S SOMEONE I WANT YOU TO MEET.
WELL, HELLO. A NEW SISTER?
MAYBE. YOU MAKE SURE HE KNOWS WHO FOUND HER IF THE ANSWER IS YES.
LOOK AT THE EYES. SHE'S SPECIAL.
SHE CERTAINLY IS. WHAT'S YOUR NAME?
MOLLY. MY NAME IS MOLLY.
WELL THEN MOLLY...
"...MEET YOUR NEW SISTERS."

SHE'S *INTACT*.
I KNOW IT FEELS WEIRD, BUT WE HAD TO KNOW YOU WERE FRESH AND CLEAN FOR HIM.
YOU'RE GOING TO MEET HIM. TO SEE HIM, ALONE. YOU BE *GRATEFUL*, NOT MANY DO. HE IS *GOOD* TO US, MOLLY...
...BE GOOD TO *HIM*.

WELL, COME ON THEN.
SHOW ME.
LOOK AT ME.

BEAUTIFUL.
THERE.
DO YOU KNOW THAT THERE ARE PEOPLE WHO *HATE* THIS WORLD?
THAT HATE THE SPREAD.
I THINK IT'S BECAUSE THEY WANT THE OLD RULES. THE OLD *SAFETY*. BUT THIS IS A *NEW* WORLD.
THIS IS MY WORLD. AND I CAN MAKE IT ANYTHING THAT I WANT. THERE ARE NO RULES BUT *MINE*.
I *LOVE* IT HERE. I LOVE THIS WORLD.
I THINK PERHAPS THOSE ASSHOLES OF THE *RISEN GOD* ARE RIGHT. I THINK...
...THIS IS *HEAVEN*.

HOW LONG?
I DON'T KNOW--
HOW LONG HAS IT BEEN SINCE YOU HAD YOUR TIME?
ALMOST A MONTH, NOT THAT IT'S--
YOU'RE LYING.
AND IT *IS* MY BUSINESS.
EVERYTHING THAT HAPPENS IN THAT TENT IS MY BUSINESS AND YOU ***WILL NOT*** LIE TO ME AGAIN.
TWO MONTHS. I THINK.
I SEE.
WHAT ARE YOU GOING TO DO?

YOU SHOULDN'T BE HERE.
THERE'S NO PLACE ELSE.
WHAT'S WRONG? DID THEY HURT YOU?
DID SOMEONE **TALK** TO YOU?
DID--
WHERE ARE THE CHILDREN?
I--WHAT?
THERE ARE NO **CHILDREN** HERE.
WELL, YEAH, DOES THIS STRIKE YOU AS A PLACE FOR CHILDREN?
YOU'RE PREGNANT.
THERE **SHOULD** BE CHILDREN. PEOPLE... MAKE LOVE ALL THE TIME. BUT THERE ARE NO CHILDREN HERE.
NO **BABIES** HERE.
WHERE ARE THE CHILDREN, RACHEL?

I'M SORRY, SISTERS.

IT WAS A GOOD PLAN.
THE FIRE DISTRACTS EVERYONE, AND MAYBE THEY THINK YOU DIED IN THE FIRE LONG ENOUGH FOR YOU TO GET FAR, FAR AWAY.
MAYBE THEY NEVER REALIZE.
I'M IMPRESSED. I HONESTLY DIDN'T THINK YOU WERE THAT SMART. BUT IT DIDN'T WORK.
BUT IF YOU COME BACK NOW, NO ONE WILL EVER KNOW YOU WENT.
NO.
THAT WAS NOT A QUESTION. AND I'M GETTING BORED.
I WON'T LET YOU.
YOU'VE DONE ENOUGH TO ME. I WON'T LET YOU DO IT TO MY BABY.
DONE ENOUGH TO YOU? I SAVED YOU.
I STOPPED SOME ASSHOLE FROM FUCKING YOU TO DEATH AND I GAVE YOU A PLACE.
DO YOU WANT ME TO THANK YOU?
FOR WHAT HE DID?
YOU THINK I DON'T KNOW? I FOUGHT MY WAY OUT OF THAT TENT. BUT THIS IS BETTER. THIS IS BETTER. WE'RE SAFE AND WE'RE STRONG.
BETTER ONE OF US THAN ONE OF THEM.
AND YOU, YOU LITTLE CUNT, YOU ARE MY RESPONSIBILITY.
AND YOU ARE GOING BACK.
NO.

NO.
NO.
NO!
NO.

SHH, SHHH.
THANK YOU.

GOING TO HAVE TO FIND A NAME FOR BABY SOMETIME.
GUBBA!
NOT ESPECIALLY HELPFUL, BABY.
KRNCH
DON'T.
PLEASE.

WE GOT A STRAGGLER.
WELL, TWO.
AND YOU NEED MY ORDER TO KNOW YOU SHOULD--
MOLLY.
FUCK.

GOOD LUCK OUTRUNNING THIS.
NO. NOT LIKE THAT.
NOT BY YOU.

FUCK!
JESUS!
FUCKING CLEVER, GIRL.
NOT NEARLY ENOUGH. I'M GOING TO...

...FIND YOU?
YOU CAN'T HIDE, MOLLY. YOU KNOW YOU CAN'T.
NOT FROM US. NOT FOREVER.
WE'RE GOING TO FIND YOU. AND I AM GOING TO LEAVE YOUR LITTLE FUCKER FOR THE SPREAD, AND I AM GOING TO CUT EVERY PIECE OF YOU OFF AND WATCH YOU STARVE.
THAT IS YOUR FUCKING FUTURE, MOLLY.
SOONER OR LATER, THAT IS YOUR FUTURE.
SHSHSH.
MMMM.

I'M SORRY, I'M SORRY.
I COULDN'T LET HER HEAR. I COULDN'T LET HER. I'M SORRY.
NO.
I'M SORRY.

MOLLY IS SORRY.

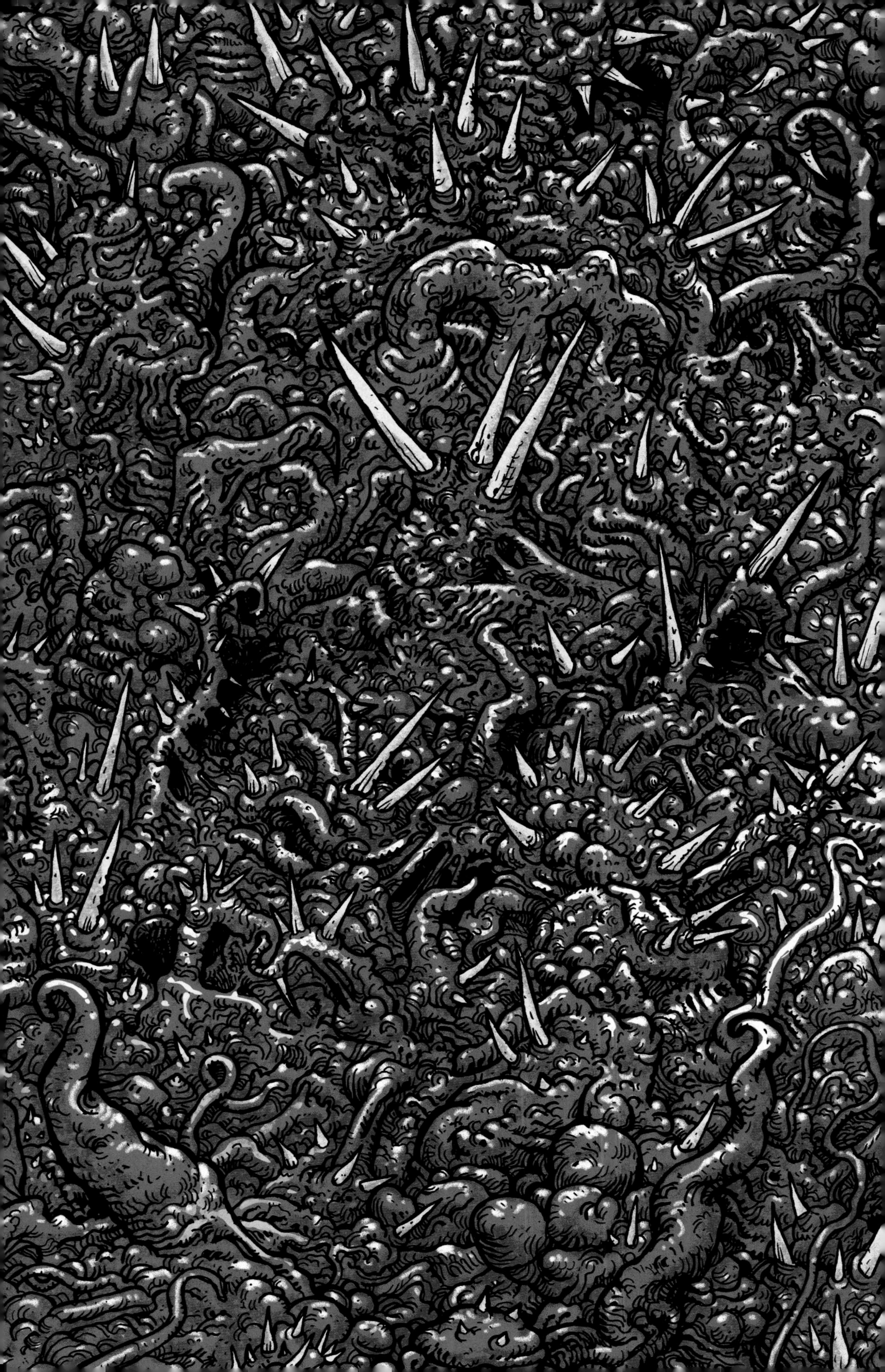

CHAPTER TWO

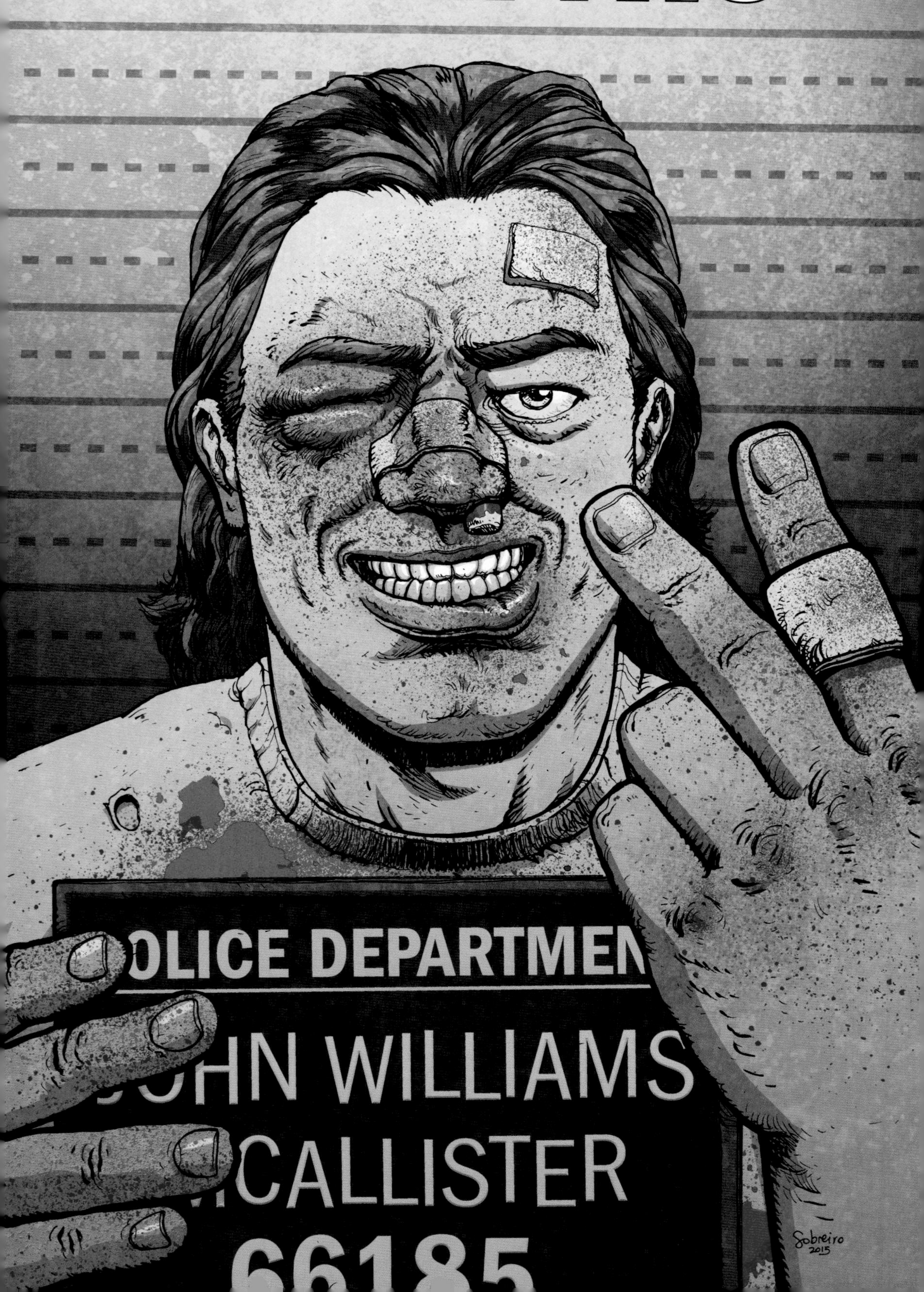
OLICE DEPARTMEN
OHN WILLIAMS
CALLISTER
66185
Sobreiro 2015

I SUPPOSE THIS IS AS GOOD A PLACE AS ANY TO START MY STORY. CERTAINLY SUMS UP MY EARLY DAYS QUITE WELL.
YOU HAVE ANYTHING TO SAY NOW, YOU FAT LITTLE FUCK?
IRON MAIDEN TOUR '83
YEAH.
FUCK YOU, MONTY.
FUCKING FAT FUCKING FUCK CUNT.
ARE YOU INTENDING TO CONTINUE THIS LIE-DOWN INDEFINITELY, JACKIE...
IRON MAIDEN

...OR WERE YOU PLANNING ON *EVER* GETTING UP?
I DON'T SUPPOSE THERE'S MUCH POINT IN ASKING WHO DID THIS TO YOU.
I WON'T SAY.
THEY'RE *NOT* YOUR MATES, JACKIE. THEY'LL ONLY DRAG YOU DOWN.
I'M *NOT* SAYING. THEY DIDN'T MEAN ANYTHING BY IT.
I WISH THAT WERE TRUE. I DO.
BUT STILL, IT'S GOOD YOU WON'T SAY. YOU'RE GOING TO BE A STAND-UP MAN SOMEDAY, JACKIE.
THEY WON'T BE ABLE TO DO THIS TO ME MUCH LONGER.
NO, I DON'T IMAGINE THEY WILL. YOU'VE GOT THE *MCALLISTER* LOOK ABOUT YOU AND WE'RE STRONG.
MY FATHER WAS A GOOD MAN. MAYBE THE BEST I EVER KNEW.
HE HAD A GOOD JOB ONCE, WITH BRITISH STEEL. BUT WHEN THE CUTS CAME, HE WAS FIRST ON THE CHOPPING BLOCK.
AND THERE WERE MOUTHS TO FEED, SO HE DID TRY.

HE TOOK WHATEVER JOBS HE COULD.
AND I HELPED HIM WHENEVER I COULD.
BUT I WATCHED A GOOD AND DECENT MAN GET FUCKED BY THE WORLD AT EVERY TURN.
CONCRETE
CONCRETE
I DID AS CHILDREN DO, AND GREW AND HELPED AS I COULD.
WHICH, AS IT HAPPENED, SOON ENDED UP BEING QUITE A LOT, AS DAD WAS RIGHT...
...I ENDED UP **STRONG**. WORK AND TIME DID THAT. AND I WAS ALWAYS SMART.
FOR HIS SAKE, I WISH I COULD TELL YOU I DID SOMETHING GOOD WITH IT.

I DIDN'T.
YOU HAVE ANYTHING ELSE TO SAY, MONTY?
PLEASE.
I THOUGHT AS MUCH.
STOP RIGHT THERE.
HOW ABOUT YOU MAKE ME?
PIGGY.
POLICE
AS IT HAPPENS, THEY WERE HAPPY TO OBLIGE ME THERE.
THIS WOULD BE A VALUABLE LESSO WHEN I WAS SMART ENOUGH TO LEARN IT: NUMBERS ALWAYS WIN.

WELL, ARE YOU JUST GOING TO SIT THERE, JACKIE?
OR ARE YOU GOING TO GET UP?
DAD, I--
NO. NOT HERE.
I'M SORRY.
NO YOU AREN'T.
SORRY I'M MAD, MAYBE, BUT NOT SORRY FOR WHAT YOU DID.
YOU'RE LUCKY, JACKIE, THAT MONTY AND HIS BOYS *ARE* AS BIG A SHITSTAINS AS *YOU* SEEM BENT ON BECOMING.
THE POLICE DON'T MUCH CARE THAT YOU PUT THEM IN THE *A AND E.*
BUT HAD THAT BEEN ONE OF THE COPS, THINGS WOULD HAVE BEEN VERY DIFFERENT.
I'M SORRY.
YOU'RE A MAN NOW, JACK, OR NEAR ENOUGH. I CAN'T TELL YOU WHAT TO DO.
BUT I CAN TELL YOU THIS: YOU'VE NO FUTURE HERE.
YOU DO WHAT YOU'VE BEEN DOING, AND THAT EITHER ENDS WITH YOU IN PRISON OR THE GRAVE.
AND HE WAS RIGHT. I KNEW THAT. SO I TOOK THE ONLY OPTION CLASSICALLY AVAILABLE TO POOR MISCREANTS AND DELINQUENTS.

I JOINED UP.
I OUGHT NOT TO HAVE BEEN ABLE TO JOIN THE ROYAL MARINES, BUT I WAS SMART AND STRONG AND YOUNG, WHICH COUNTED FOR QUITE A LOT.
I'M NOT SURE **FUN** IS THE RIGHT WORD. BUT I **LIKED** IT.
ACTUALLY APPLIED MYSELF FOR THE FIRST TIME.
AND REAPED THE REWARDS.
I WAS A LEGIT MEMBER OF SOCIETY.

THAT'S NOT TO SAY IT WAS ALL ROSES AND SUNSHINE.
I DID GET SENT TO EVERY FUCKING **SHITPIT** THE WORLD COULD OFFER. BUT STILL...
...IT HAD ITS MOMENTS.
COME ON IF YOU THINK YOU'RE **HARD** ENOUGH!
AND YOU BELIEVE THEY'RE GIVING ME A BLOODY MEDAL? **HAH**.
AND SO THEY DID. DAD WAS PROUD.
DAD WAS STILL PRE-EMAIL, THOSE DAYS. SO I ACTUALLY WROTE LETTERS. THAT'S COME ROUND AGAIN, I SUPPOSE. THINGS ALWAYS DO.
Dear Mom and Dad,
LOOK AT **THE SPREAD**.

OF COURSE, THERE WAS ALSO OPPORTUNITY FOR ENTREPRENEURIAL VENTURES, AS WELL.
WELL, LAMB?
Morley
Morley
HAVANA
YOU KNOW THIS IS FUCKING OBSCENE, RIGHT?
YOU'RE FREE TO SEND YOUR MONEY ELSEWHERE.
FUCK.
HAVANA
PLEASURE DOING BUSINESS, MATE.
SMALL VENTURES AT TIMES.
BIGGER WHEN I HAD THE CHANCE.
NOTHING THAT WOULD ENDANGER CROWN AND COUNTRY, OF COURSE.

BUT ENOUGH FOR A HEALTHY PROFIT MARGIN. THAT AND A PENSION, I COULD DO WELL. JUST GET MY TIME IN.
AY, SERGEANT...
...PHONE CALL.
TA.
IT WAS A GOOD TIME, ALL IN ALL.
WHEN?
NO, I UNDERSTAND. I'M ON MY WAY.
BUT LIKE ALL GOOD THINGS...
...IT WAS NOT TO LAST.

FIFTY-TWO YEARS OLD. WORKED HARD HIS WHOLE LIFE UNTIL HE WAS AN OLD MAN TWENTY YEARS EARLY AND WHAT?
STABBED IN THE BACK DURING A FIGHT THAT WASN'T ANY OF HIS BUSINESS.
AND IN A CROWDED PUB, NOT A PERSON WHO COULD IDENTIFY THE BASTARD WHO DID IT.
IT'S GOOD YOU WERE ABLE TO COME. HE WAS SO PROUD OF YOU.
YEAH.

MY DAD WAS A GOOD AND HONEST MAN. HE TRIED. HE FUCKING WELL TRIED. HE WAS LEGIT AND ALL IT GOT HIM WAS DEAD ON A PUB FLOOR.
THIS WAS NOT MY FUTURE. WHAT I'D DO WOULD DISAPPOINT HIM, I'M SURE, BUT THEN HE WASN'T AROUND TO DISAPPOINT.
BUT I HAD THINGS TO TAKE CARE OF. NO WITNESSES FOR THE POLICE IS NOT THE SAME AS NO WITNESSES.
I FOUND THE FUCKER EASY ENOUGH.
AND TOOK CARE OF WHAT NEEDED TAKING CARE OF.
JACK?
JACKIE?

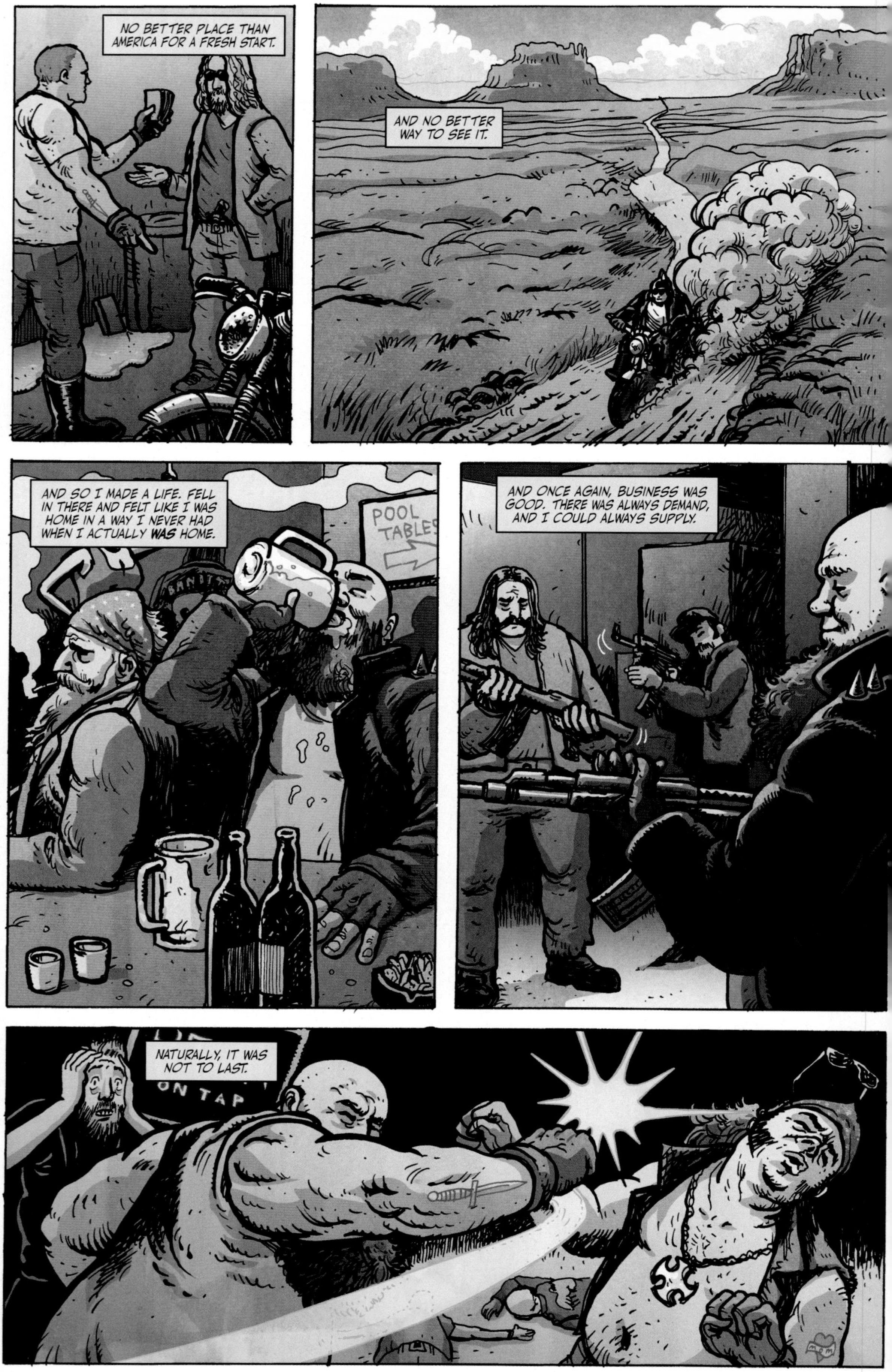
NO BETTER PLACE THAN AMERICA FOR A FRESH START.
AND NO BETTER WAY TO SEE IT.
AND SO I MADE A LIFE. FELL IN THERE AND FELT LIKE I WAS HOME IN A WAY I NEVER HAD WHEN I ACTUALLY WAS HOME.
POOL TABLES
AND ONCE AGAIN, BUSINESS WAS GOOD. THERE WAS ALWAYS DEMAND, AND I COULD ALWAYS SUPPLY.
NATURALLY, IT WAS NOT TO LAST.
ON TAP

THIS IS NOT JUST FOOLISHNESS, I HAVE TO SAY. I'D NEVER ACTUALLY INFORMED OR ASKED THE MARINES ABOUT MY RETIREMENT, SO I WAS TECHNICALLY A WANTED MAN. IT WOULDN'T DO TO BE ARRESTED.
OF COURSE, THAT PROVED TO BE A LUCKY BREAK, IN THE END. A WEEK EARLIER AND I'D HAVE BEEN DEPORTED BY THE TIME IT HAPPENED.
BUT I WAS HERE, RIGHT IN THE HEART OF THE Q.Z. IT WASN'T THE Q.Z. THEN, OF COURSE.
REAKING NEW
NOT YET.
WHAT ABOUT THEM?
FUCK THEM. WE GO NOW OR WE DON'T EVER GO.
POLICE
ONE GOOD MAN. YOU'D THINK THERE'D HAVE BEEN ONE GOOD MAN AMONG THEM, WHO'D HAVE OPENED THE DOOR FOR US.
ALTHOUGH IN RETROSPECT, I CAN HARDLY BLAME THEM.
FUCK ME.
WHICH, AS IT TURNS OUT...

...THEY HAD.
WE WERE LEFT.
THIS WAS A PROBLEM.
THEY HADN'T SUPPLIED US WITH ANYTHING TO EAT.
ALTHOUGH THERE WAS A COMPLIMENTARY BEVERAGE SERVICE, AFTER A FASHION.
BEING A MAN OF SUBSTANTIAL DIMENSIONS I HAD A CERTAIN ADVANTAGE IN THIS REGARD.
AND OF COURSE, I MADE DO WITH THE SUPPLIES AT HAND.
BUT NOTHING LASTS FOREVER.

SO, SOON ENOUGH, I WAS IN A BAD WAY.
KACHUNK
I WASN'T INCLINED TO QUESTION MY LUCK, SUCH AS IT WAS, AND I CERTAINLY WASN'T ONE TO OVERLOOK OPPORTUNITY.
AS IT HAPPENS...

I WASN'T ALONE THERE.
FUCK!
SKLATCH
FUCK FUCK FUCK.
SHUK
BASTARD.
SPLURCH
I SUGGEST YOU MOVE...

THEY *DON'T* DIE.
JESUS.
AND THAT WAS HOW I MET **MERRIWEATHER**. WELL, AND THE SPREAD AS WELL, OBVIOUSLY.
FUCKING CHRIST. IS THAT WHAT'S OUT HERE?
WOULD YOU HAVE PREFERRED I LEFT THAT CELL DOOR LOCKED?
HAH, NO. THANK YOU FOR THAT.
I'M JACK.
DO YOU HAVE A NAME?
I DO. BUT I'M WAITING TO SEE IF YOU'RE GOING TO CHANGE.
INTO WHAT?
THAT.
THAT WAS A FUCKING PERSON?
ONCE. THE SPREAD INFECTS ***EVERYTHING***. PEOPLE, ANIMALS, PLANTS.
AND I'M LIKELY TO CHANGE INTO ***THAT?***
APPARENTLY NOT.
MERRIWEATHER. IT'S A PLEASURE TO MEET YOU.

THIS WAS INDEED THE START OF A BEAUTIFUL FRIENDSHIP, OR AT LEAST, A FRUITFUL BUSINESS PARTNERSHIP.
WE BOOTSTRAPPED UP.
AND WE MADE AN INTERESTING DISCOVERY.
ONE QUITE A LOT OF PEOPLE WOULD MAKE. WE COULD USE THE SPREAD AS A WEAPON. MERRI AND I, BEING AMONGST THE LUCKY FEW TO BE SPREAD IMMUNE, COULD ROB THOSE THAT WEREN'T AND THEY WOULDN'T DARE FOLLOW US NEAR THE SPREAD.
THAT WAS USEFUL INFORMATION. ESPECIALLY ONCE WE FOUND SOME LIKE-MINDED FELLOWS TO PARTNER UP WITH.

OF COURSE, WE WEREN'T THE ONLY ONES WHO FOUND A WAY TO PROFIT FROM BEING ABLE AND WILLING TO GO WHERE OTHERS WOULDN'T.
THE SALVAGEMEN (AND, ACTUALLY QUITE A FEW WOMEN) STARTED COMING NORTH. GO INTO THE SPREAD, GET WHAT WAS VALUABLE, GO SOUTH AND TRADE.
THIS, AS SUCH THINGS DO, GAVE ME AN IDEA.
I CAN SEE YOU THINKING, JACK.
INDEED I AM.
MERRI MY FRIEND, LET ME TELL YOU ABOUT THE FUTURE.

OF COURSE, BUILDING THE FUTURE REQUIRED MANPOWER.
WHICH LEAD TO MERRI'S NEW JOB. HE WAS IN H.R. BEFORE, SO PROCURING AND MANAGING **HUMAN** RESOURCES PROVED TO BE A NATURAL FIT.
I WAS LESS KEEN ON THAT, BUT BUSINESS WAS BUSINESS, YEAH? SO WE BUILT.
MY IDEA WAS SIMPLE: BUILD A PLACE WHERE THOSE WHO WERE ABLE TO PROFIT FROM THE SPREAD COULD TRADE FREE AND SAFE WITH THOSE WHO WERE NOT.
SPAM
AND INDEED, IT PROVED TO BE QUITE A **POPULAR** CONCEPT.
JACK'S

OF COURSE, THE CAMP HAD TO BE MOBILE. THE SPREAD, AFTER ALL, DID JUST THAT IN ITS IRREGULAR AND UNPREDICTABLE WAY.
AND OF COURSE, THERE WERE OTHER CONSIDERATIONS MORE MUNDANE. TREATIES MADE.
BARGAINS HAD. BUT ALL IN ALL...
...LIFE WAS GOOD FOR YOUR JACKIE.
COOK

VERY GOOD.
BUT NOTHING LASTS FOREVER. NOT BEFORE AND CERTAINLY NOT NOW.
ALL RIGHT...
...LET'S SEE ABOUT DINNER.
PLEASE, NO.
I'D TELL YOU IT'S NOT PERSONAL, MATE, BUT HONESTLY IT KIND OF IS.
YOU KNOW THE RULES ABOUT FIGHTING IN THE CAMP AND RILING UP THE NUTTERS, AND YET--

GOT A MESSAGE, BOSS.
NOT IN FRONT OF THE *MEAT*.
HE LOST *FIVE* MEN?
THE SPREAD'S PERKED UP AGAIN. IT'S MOVING THIS WAY.
WE LOST ANOTHER TWO AND A CART TO A *SPREADWORM*.
FUCK.
IF THERE'S *ONE* SPREADWORM, THERE WILL BE *MORE*. TIME TO MOVE AGAIN.
TELL MERRI HE HAS MY THANKS. HAVE SOME *CHILI* IF YOU LIKE.
ALWAYS BLOODY SOMETHING.
YOU KNOW...

...THERE'S ONLY *ME* SUPPOSED TO BE IN HERE.
ACE
AND **THAT**, OF COURSE, WAS HOW I MET YOUR **FATHER**.

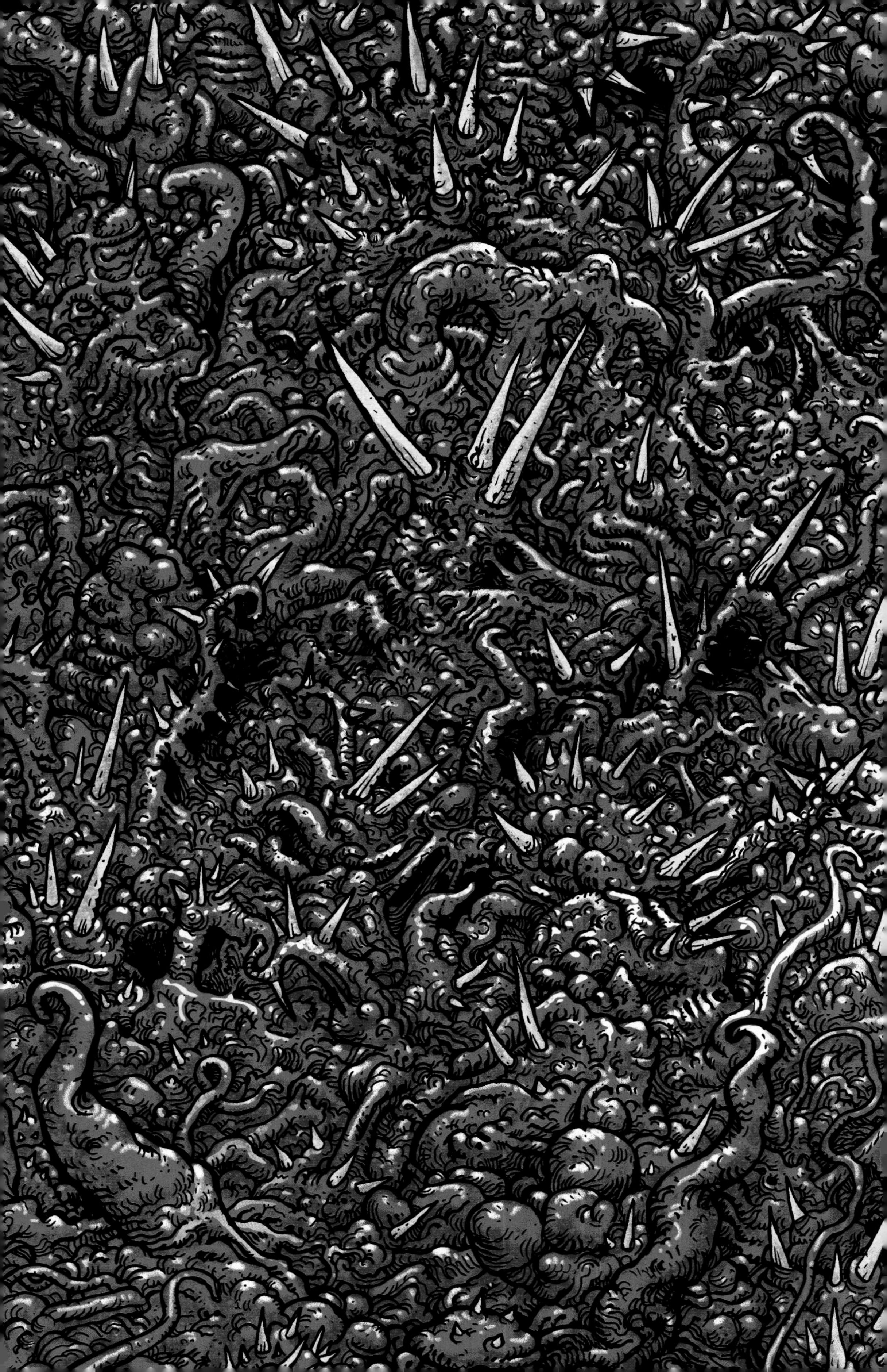

CHAPTER THREE

HOW IS HE?
NNNN...
SHHHH, IT'S OKAY. WE'RE ALMOST THERE.
PAM.
HE'S STILL ALIVE. HE'S...

HE'S GOING TO MAKE IT.
THEY HAVE MEDICINE. THEY CAN HELP US.
WE'RE LESS THAN A DAY OUT BY WHAT HE TOLD US.
YOU HEAR YOUR DAD? JUST A LITTLE FARTHER AND YOU'LL BE ALL BETTER.
JUST HOLD ON, OKAY?
OH.
OH NO.

MOM?
ELLIE?

WELL, HELLO THERE.
I AM SORRY...
...BUT WE HAVE A JOB TO DO.

NO.
NO.
NO!

I WOULDN'T.
YOU WERE IN A BAD WAY. YOU'RE STILL ON I.V. ANTIBIOTICS.
SO PULLING THAT I.V. OUT IS A BAD IDEA.

I DID SEE THIS. NOT THAT I REMEMBER. I ONLY KNOW WHAT THEY TOLD ME ABOUT IT. I ONLY KNOW THAT FOR A LITTLE BIT, MOLLY WAS **HAPPY**.

CIVILIZATION DOES HAVE ITS RISKS.
MOLLY IS SORRY.
NO.
SHE STILL HASN'T GOTTEN THE HANG OF THAT.
SHE WAS ONLY EIGHT WHEN THE SPREAD CAME, SO HER CAR REFLEXES ARE A LITTLE ATROPHIED.
ARE YOU OKAY?
MOLLY IS FINE. HOPE IS FINE.
ARE YOU OKAY?

MOLLY LIKES IT HERE.
OKAY.
HOW--?
BIODIESEL.
GAS DOESN'T LAST A DECADE, AND NEW VEHICLES' ELECTRONICS GOT FRIED BY THE BURN.
THAT WAS THE QUESTION, YEAH? HOW IS THERE A TRUCK?
YES.
HARD WORK.
OLD VEHICLES, ONES FROM THE SIXTIES AND SEVENTIES, WERE PRETTY MUCH IMMUNE TO E.M.
ONCE WE WERE ABLE TO GET THE BIODIESEL MADE, IT WAS JUST A MATTER OF TIME.
WE'VE GOT ELECTRICITY TOO, SOMETIMES. WORKING ON SEWERAGE.
IF YOU SQUINT, IT ALMOST LOOKS LIKE THE REAL WORLD.
SANCTUARY.
ALL RIGHT, SORRY, I'VE GOT THINGS TO DO-- ALWAYS THINGS TO DO--AND YOU GUYS DEFINITELY NEED SOME TOGETHER TIME.
BUT I'M AROUND IF YOU NEED ME.
IT WAS PARADOX. IT SHOWED THEM AGAIN THE WORLD WASN'T LIKE THEY THOUGHT.

AND THAT IT WAS.
SO HE'S AWAKE.
HE IS.
WHICH MEANS?
I DON'T KNOW.
HE WON'T WANT TO STAY. WE CAN'T LET HER GO.
CAN'T WE?
YOU KNOW WE CAN'T. AND IT'S JUST A MATTER OF TIME BEFORE IT KNOWS SHE'S HERE.
WHY DOESN'T IT ALREADY? IT'S CLOSE ENOUGH.
I DON'T THINK IT CAN SMELL HER. SHE'S A BLINDSPOT.
BUT IT'S NOT DUMB, AND IT'S GETTING SMARTER. AND SO WE'RE GOING TO HAVE TO MAKE A DECISION.
SO THIS IS A WE THING?
YOU GOING TO FIGHT ME ON THIS? I KNOW YOU AND MOLLY HAVE HISTORY.
DO YOU NOW?
I'M NOT DUMB EITHER. I KEEP LOOKING FOR A WAY TO SAVE HER AND US. AND I'M NOT SEEING IT.
BUT IF YOU GOT A BETTER IDEA, PLEASE FILL ME IN.
...

I DON'T LIKE IT.
WHICH PART?
ANY PART.
WELL...
CONSIDER YOUR ALTERNATIVES. WE ***DO THIS*** AND ***PROBABLY*** DIE, OR ***WE RUN*** AND WE ***DEFINITELY*** DIE.
THERE AREN'T ANY GOOD OPTIONS.
DOESN'T MEAN I HAVE TO ***LIKE*** IT.
HEY...
WE GOT...

...TROUBLE.
ONLY IF YOU ASK FOR IT.
HANDS, PLEASE.
WE NEED HELP FOR OUR BOY.
THAT MAN, THE PROFESSOR, HE SAID SANCTUARY COULD HELP.
STAY WHERE YOU ARE, SIR, AND WE'LL SEE WHAT WE CAN SEE.
HRRRM.
HELLO, LOVELY.

FUCK!
MAL!
SIR, DON'T MOVE.
WHAT.
THE.
FUCK?!

HAH!
NOW LET'S SEE ABOUT YOU.

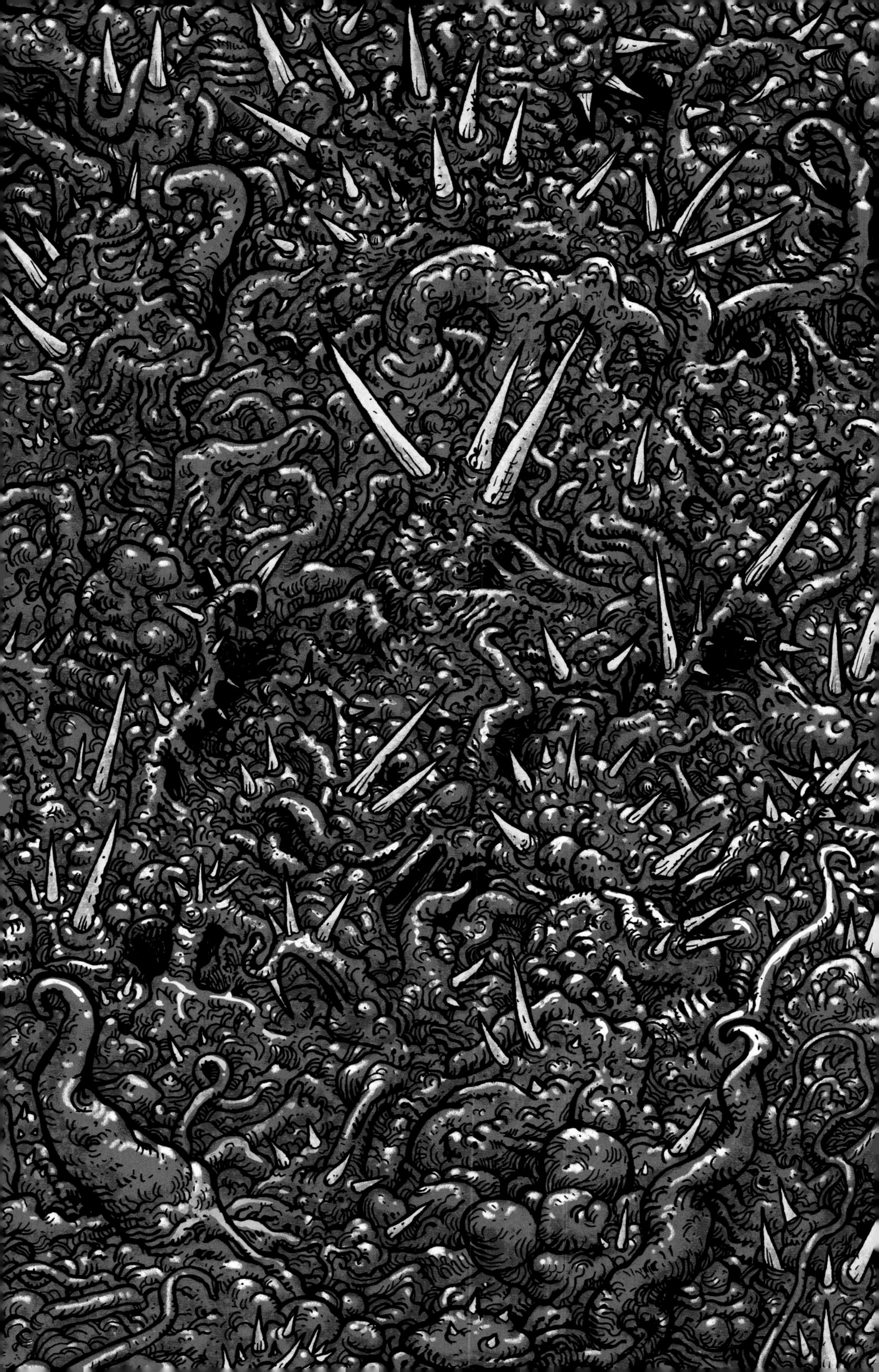

CHAPTER FOUR

CLANG CLANG CLANG
HE WASN'T A BAD MAN.
CLANG CLANG CLANG
CAMERON.
CLANG CLANG CLANG
I REALIZE YOU'RE GOING TO HAVE A HARD TIME WITH THAT, ESPECIALLY COMING FROM ME.
WHAT THE ACTUAL HELL?
CLANG CLANG CLANG
BUT HE WAS A GOOD MAN.
IT WAS THE WORLD THAT WAS BAD.
CLANG CLANG CLANG

CLANG
SOMETHING THAT NO NEVER, EVER FORGOT.
IS THIS YOURS?
THIS WORKSHOP?
CLANG
YES.
I SUPPOSE SO. THIS VEHICLE, HAVE YOU SEEN ONE BEFORE?
YES.
BUT THAT, AS THEY SAY, WAS A STORY FOR ANOTHER TIME.

THERE'S A FEW AROUND, FROM WHEN THE GOVERNMENT WAS ACTUALLY BOTHERING TO TRY AND SAVE US.
IT'D BEEN ABANDONED FOR YEARS, OF COURSE, BUT IT WAS A PLACE TO BEGIN. SOMEPLACE SAFE TO START.
WHY?
WHY?
WHY ARE YOU HERE?
WHY IS THIS PLACE HERE?
BECAUSE IT SHOULD BE.
THERE SHOULD BE A SAFE PLACE, SOMEWHERE.
YOU DON'T BELIEVE THAT?
...

I BELIEVE IN THIS.
OF COURSE YOU DO. WOULD IT DO ME ANY GOOD TO TELL YOU THAT YOU WON'T NEED THAT HERE?
NO.
BECAUSE YOU'RE NOT PLANNING ON STAYING.
YOU PLAN TO LEAVE.
WHY NOT STAY?
WHY NOT BE PART OF SOMETHING?
WHY NOT GIVE MOLLY AND HOPE A SAFE PLACE?

THERE IS NO SAFE PLACE.
BUT WHAT IF THERE COULD BE? WHAT IF WE BUILD SOMETHING THAT COULD LAST?
YOU CAN'T. THE SPREAD WILL DO WHAT THE SPREAD DOES. IT WILL TAKE EVERYTHING.
I DON'T THINK THAT HAS TO BE TRUE. I DON'T THINK WE UNDERSTAND THE SPREAD AT ALL.
AND THAT WAS TRUE. WE REALLY, REALLY DIDN'T.
WHAT IF IT COULD THINK? WHAT IF THE SPREAD IS INTELLIGENT, BUT ITS MIND IS SPREAD OUT OVER TENS OF THOUSANDS OF SQUARE MILES OF BIOMASS? SMART, BUT SLOW.
WHAT IF WE COULD TALK TO IT? HAVE YOU EVER EVEN CONSIDERED THAT? HOPED FOR THAT? THAT THERE COULD BE PEACE.
NO.

IT WASN'T JUST THE FUTURE OCCUPYING THEIR MINDS THEN.
THE PAST NEEDED TO MAKE AN APPEARANCE TOO.
HELLO.
SHIT.

OLD HABIT.
IN ANY CASE, THESE TWO CLAIM TO HAVE BEEN SENT HERE BY THE PROFESSOR TO GET HELP FOR THEIR CHILD.
AND THAT MERITS THIS?
THAT? NO. THE CACHE OF WEAPONS THEY HAD HID IN THE WAGON DID THAT. I SUSPECT OUR LOVELY COUPLE WAS TRYING TO TROJAN HORSE THIS PLACE.
AND YOU BROUGHT THEM INSIDE INSTEAD OF LETTING US HANDLE THIS THE WAY WE HANDLE IT?
BETTER OUT THAN IN, EH?

PLEASE, WE NEED HELP.
WE NEED SANCTUARY.
WAS THAT NECESSARY?
I CERTAINLY THOUGHT SO. BUT THEN, IT'S NOT FOR ME TO JUDGE, IS IT?
NO. THAT, UNFORTUNATELY, IS MY JOB.
I'D LIKE TO APOLOGIZE. WE HAVE TO BE CAREFUL.
THIS WORLD IS NOT THE PLACE WE'D LIKE IT TO BE.
PLEASE, PLEASE, OUR BOY... HE'S SICK.
HE'S REAL SICK, YOU GOT TO HELP US.

NO.
I'M SORRY.
WE'LL GIVE YOU A HOT MEAL AND A SAFE SPACE. AFTER THAT, WE'LL SEE.
I HOPE YOU CAN STAY, BUT HOPE... JUST ISN'T ENOUGH.

YEAH...
...I THOUGHT YOU'D BE HAPPY TO SEE ME.
OR NOT.
YOU KNOW, I PACK-MULED YOUR ARSE FOR A HUNDRED MILES.
YOU'D THINK A LITTLE GRATITUDE WOULD BE IN ORDER.
NO.
SO, WHEN ARE YOU PLANNING ON LEAVING?

I DON'T LIKE THIS PLACE EITHER. AND TO BE FAIR, ***THEY*** DON'T LIKE ***ME***. IT'S AS IF THEY FEEL I'M NOT TRUSTWORTHY.
...
ALL RIGHT, FAIR, BUT ***THEY'VE*** NO REASON TO THINK THAT. IT'S INSULTING. THAT'S WHY I'M BEING SENT OUT ON GUARD DUTY.
THEY DON'T WANT OL' JACK ***INSIDE***. I FIGURE THEY HOPE I'LL GET KILLED OR WANDER OFF.
WHY HAVEN'T YOU?
OH, HE ***SPEAKS!*** A FULL SENTENCE, EVEN. WHAT A JOYOUS DAY.
...
I AM GLAD TO SEE YOUR SENSE OF HUMOR IS INTACT. ANYWAY, THE ANSWER IS THE SAME AS WHY YOU'RE HERE...
...***THEM***.
SHE DOESN'T WANT TO LEAVE.
NO, SHE DOES NOT. AND I'M NOT SURE THEY'RE INCLINED TO ***LET*** HER.
AND SEEING AS THERE IS A DISTINCT LACK OF TRUST, I DOUBT THEY'D LET ME TAKE HER.
AND YOU THINK I WANT TO LEAVE.
OH, I ***KNOW*** THAT. I KNEW YOU'D SMELL IT AS SOON AS YOU REJOINED THE LIVING.
THIS PLACE ISN'T RIGHT. THIS IMPOSSIBLE PLACE.
WON'T LAST. ***CAN'T*** LAST.
I'D PREFER TO BE GONE WHEN IT DOESN'T.
I'M DUE BACK OUTSIDE THE GATES, BUT I'M GOING TO WANDER OFF TONIGHT, IF YOU'D CARE TO JOIN ME.
IF YOU CAN GET OVER THE WALL.
THERE WAS ONE THING THAT WAS DEFINITELY TRUE IN THE WORLD THE SPREAD MADE...

...PARANOIA IS A SURVIVAL STRATEGY.
ARE YOU READY?
JESUS, BIV, JUST FUCKING DO IT.
I'M SORRY.
PUSS--
YOU NEED TO HELP US, I THINK SHE'S GOT THE SAME THING AS OUR BOY.
SHE'S BLEEDING.
SHIT.

BOB, YOU NEED TO GET CAMERON.
BOB?
EVEN EASIER THAN EXPECTED.
BOB!
WOULDN'T WORRY ABOUT BOB.

HELLO, CAN ANYBODY HEAR ME?
THIS NEXT PART...
...WELL, IT'S GOING TO MAKE THAT **GOOD MAN** BIT HARD TO SWALLOW.
=SIGH=
HELLO, CAN ANYONE HEAR ME?
KLIK
OH, YES...
...**WE** CAN HEAR YOU.
MAY I TURN AROUND?
SURE. I'D LIKE TO SEE THE LOOK ON YOUR FACE.

I GUESS JACK WAS RIGHT ABOUT YOU.
I WISH THAT WEREN'T SO.
WASN'T OUR CHOICE. WHAT'S OUT THERE, YOU CAN'T IMAGINE.
HE TOLD US TO COME HERE AND OPEN THE WAY. I FIGURED WE'D PROBABLY DIE, BUT I ASSURE YOU, IT *IS* BETTER THAN THE ALTERNATIVE.
BUT WE GOT **LUCKY**. YOU LEAVE YOUR DOOR OPEN.
YOU ***DIDN'T*** GET LUCKY.
I JUST WISH YOU HADN'T HURT THOSE MEN. THEY WERE GOOD PEOPLE.
YEAH, WELL, SEE WHERE ***GOOD*** GETS YOU.
KLIK
KLIK
WHAT THE FUCK?!
I'M ***NOT*** A GOOD MAN. AND THIS...
YEAH.
BUT REMEMBER, THINGS CAN **ALWAYS** GET WORSE.
NO. WE'RE ***PROTECTED!***
...THIS WAS A TEST.

"YOU FAILED."

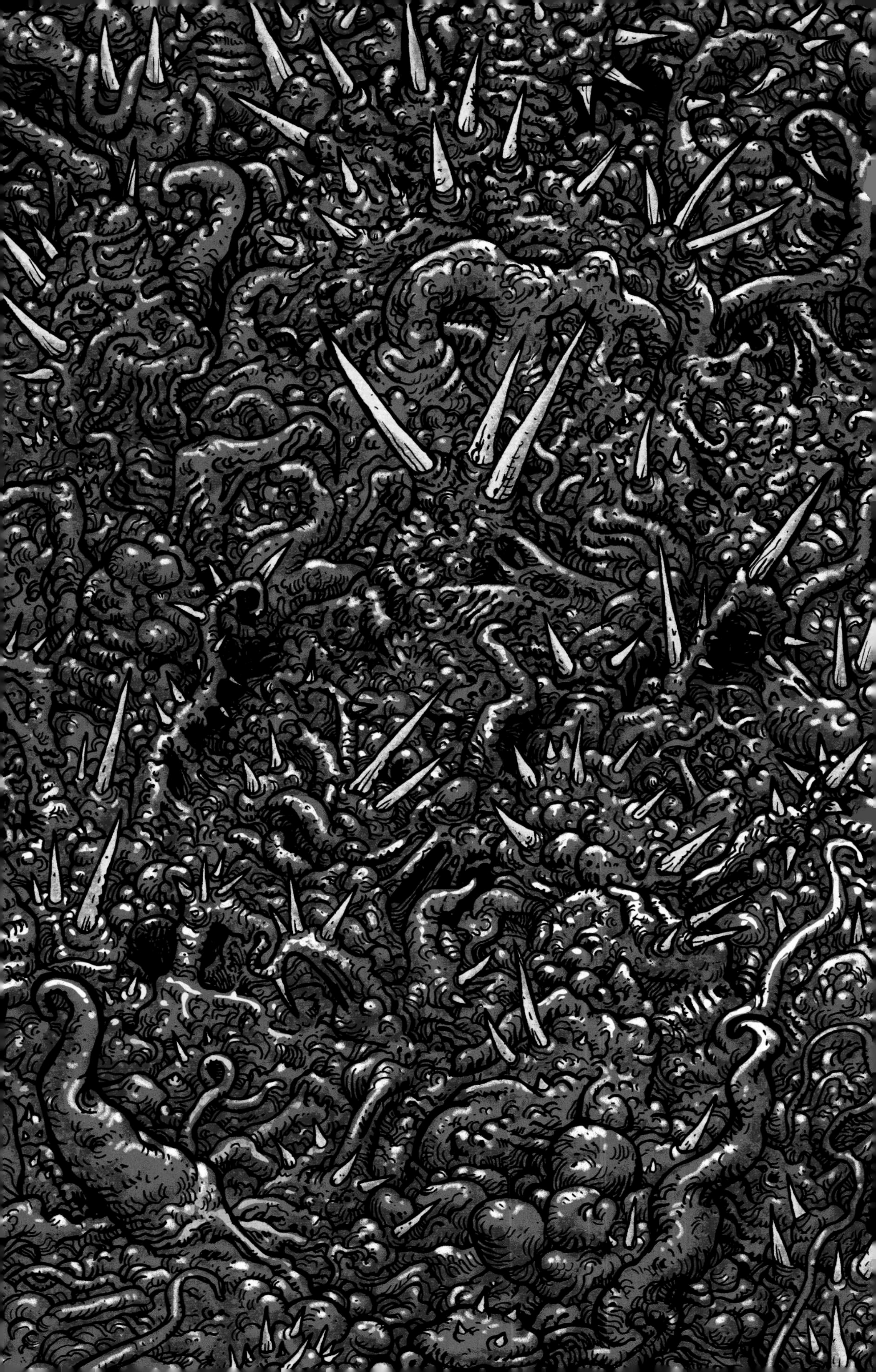

CHAPTER FIVE

I ASSUME YOU KILLED THE GUARDS.
THAT WASN'T NECESSARY.
THEN AGAIN, I'M NOT SURE *ANY* OF THIS IS.
I WISH I COULD MAKE YOU *SEE* THAT.

I WISH IT WASN'T THIS WAY.
WE CAN MAKE PEACE WITH IT.
YOU DON'T UNDERSTAND WHAT IT IS. WHAT SANCTUARY IS.
THE SPREAD ISN'T STUPID. BUT IT IS LARGE.
IMAGINE A SINGLE INTELLIGENCE SPREAD OVER A BIOMASS THAT COVERS HUNDREDS OF THOUSANDS OF SQUARE MILES.
BILLIONS OF TONS OF BRAIN.

CAPABLE OF IMMENSE THOUGHT, BUT ONLY CAPABLE OF THINKING SLOWLY. BUT IT'S GETTING FASTER.
IT'S GENERATING CENTRALIZED INTELLIGENCES... PIECES OF IT SMALL ENOUGH TO INTERACT WITH US.
SYMBIOSIS.
THAT IS WHAT SANCTUARY IS.
PROOF OF CONCEPT.
IT PROTECTS US. WE TEACH IT.
THIS IS THE FUTURE. AND WE HAVE TO KEEP THE FUTURE SAFE.

"NO MATTER WHAT THE COST."
SANCTUARY WAS AN IMPOSSIBLE PLACE.
IT WAS ALSO A DANGEROUS PLACE.

SHHH SHH SHH.
I NEED VERY MUCH FOR YOU NOT TO SCREAM.
YES.

SO DO I.
I'M NOT ENTIRELY SURE **NO** EVER ACTUALLY **SLEPT**, NOW THAT YOU MENTION IT.
I DON'T MEAN ANY HARM.
I MIGHT.
DON'T HURT THE BABY.
I WON'T. I **CAN'T**.
THAT'S WHY I'M HERE.
IT'S GOT TO BE ABOUT MORE THAN JUST SURVIVING.
WHO ARE YOU?

I USED TO BE *YOU.*
OR SOMEONE VERY MUCH LIKE YOU.
I PROTECTED *MOLLY* FROM THIS WORLD.
UNTIL I DIDN'T.
AND NOW?
I'M NOT GOING TO ASK YOU TO TRUST ME. I HAVEN'T EARNED THAT. I'M NOT SURE IF I CAN.
BUT I WILL TELL YOU...
...YOU'RE *RIGHT*. THIS IS *NOT* A SAFE PLACE.
NOT FOR *YOU*. MAYBE NOT FOR *ANYONE*.
THEY'RE NOT GOING TO JUST LET YOU LEAVE.
BUT WE *NEED* TO GO.

I ONLY WISH...
...THIS WERE ANY SORT OF SURPRISE.
IS THIS MEANT TO BE A SNACK STOP, JACK?
OH, ISN'T HE FUNNY.
NO.
JUDGING BY THE TRACKS AND WHERE THEY ARE, I'D SAY THESE ARE THE ORIGINAL OCCUPANTS OF THE WAGON WE BROUGHT IN.
YOU BROUGHT IN.
SURE, WHY NOT?
YOU DON'T SEEM ESPECIALLY CONCERNED.
SANCTUARY IS A SAFE PLACE.
NO SUCH ANIMAL.

YOU CAN COME IF YOU LIKE, BUT I'D LEAVE YOUR NOBLE STEEDS.
I DON'T IMAGINE THEY'LL EASILY FOLLOW.
SHIT.
YEAH...

"...I'D SAY THAT JUST ABOUT SUMS IT UP."

ISN'T *THIS* A NASTY SURPRISE?

FOUR AGAINST ONE HARDLY SEEMS FAIR.
FUCK FAIR.

HAH!
KRAK
AS I SAID...
...HARDLY FAIR.
KRK
I HOPE YOU AREN'T SO FOOLISH TO THINK YOU CAN KILL ME WITH *THAT* PIGSTICKER.
THIS? NO.
BUT I THINK *THEY'VE* GOT A CHANCE.

CAMERON WAS A GOOD MAN. AND HE **WASN'T WRONG**. SO WE NEEDED TO LEAVE.
NOW, WHY DON'T YOU TELL ME...
...WHAT IT IS YOU THINK YOU'RE DOING.
DISTRICT 201
I... UH... SLEEPING.
WELL, POINTS FOR HONESTY.
GO CHECK ON THE GUESTS. THE ***NEW*** GUESTS.
I GOT THIS.
WE CAN'T MOVE THIS THING SO WE'RE GOING TO HAVE TO GO OVER.
WE DON'T HAVE LONG. I HID THE ***GUNS***, BUT STILL.
WELL...
JUST...

...EASIER SAID THAN DONE.
...THAT'S TRUE.
WHAT ARE YOU DOING, RAVEN?
YOU KNOW DAMN WELL WHAT I AM DOING.
THIS ISN'T RIGHT. NONE OF IT IS.
AND CAN YOU DROP THE DAMN DRAMA?

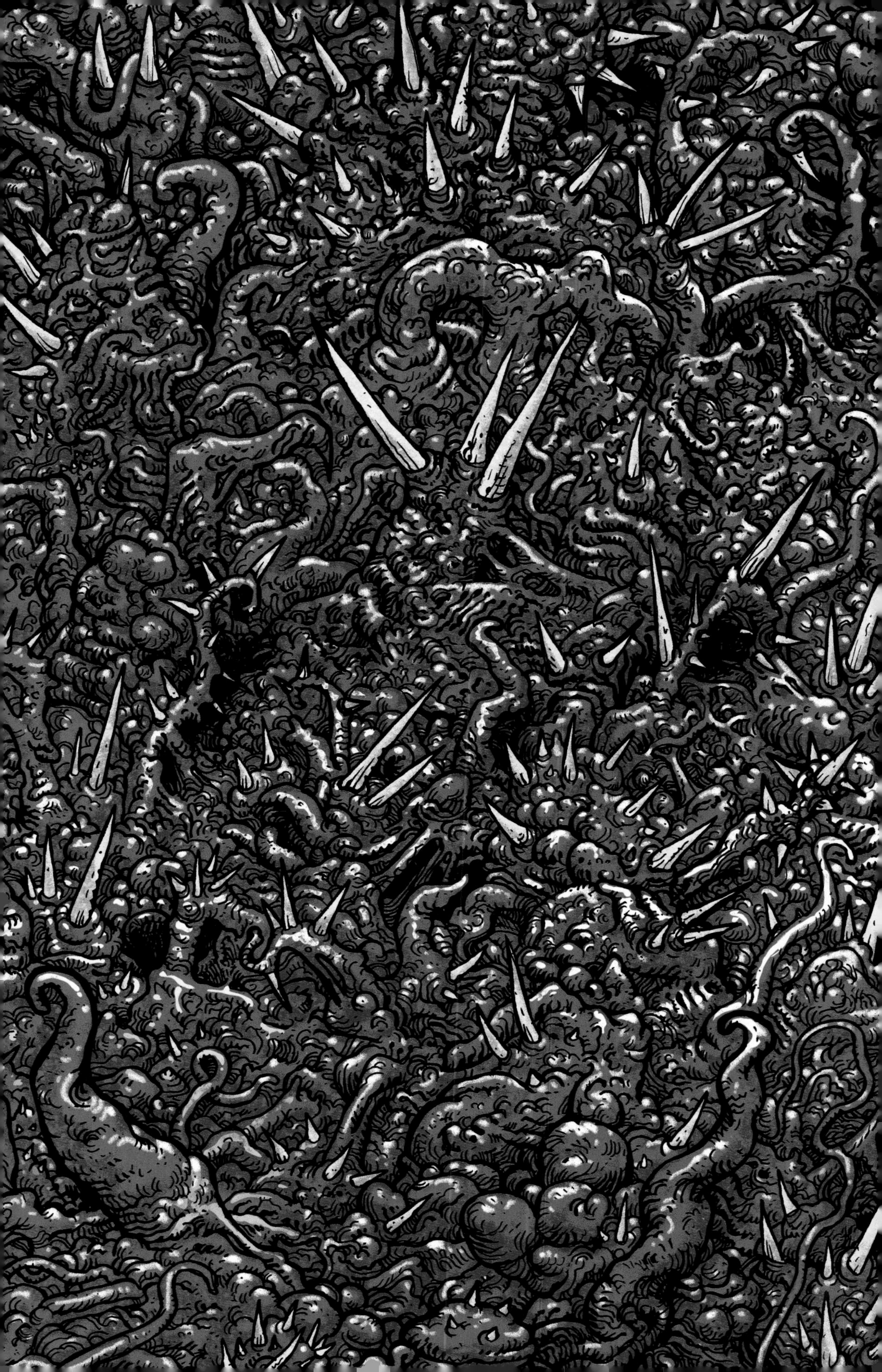

CHAPTER SIX

THIS WAS NOT, AS IT TURNED OUT, ONE OF JACK'S **BETTER** DAYS.
OH, FUCK ME.
I REALLY HOPE SO.

SHIT.
YOU DON'T STRIKE ME AS THE RIGHT KIND OF SURPRISED, DOUG.
UFFF!
WE SHOULD HAVE A CHAT ABOUT THAT.

OF COURSE, IT'LL NEED TO BE BRIEF.
WOMP
CAN'T... BREATHE.
THEN I'D NOT WASTE YOUR BREATH WHINING.
HOW IS IT THAT THOSE BEASTIES HAVE NO INTEREST IN YOU AND ME?
KNOWS... US. OUR SCENTS.
TRACKING THE SCENTS... OF PEOPLE IN WAGON.
I'D CALL THAT IMPOSSIBLE, BUT I AM LEARNING IMPOSSIBLE DOESN'T RATE LIKE IT USED TO.
SANCTUARY IS... SAFE.
OH, I DOUBT THAT VERY MUCH.
BUT THAT'S NOT YOUR PROBLEM, IS IT?
NOOO...
NOT ANYMORE.

I CAN'T HELP BUT BE CURIOUS AS TO WHAT, EXACTLY...
...IS HAPPENING OVER HILL AND DALE.
WE WERE SUPPOSED TO BE *SAFE*.
HE *SHOWED* US.

THIS IS NOT A PARTICULARLY PLEASING DEVELOPMENT.
WELL, IF MY LUCK HOLDS...
KUCK

"...NO SHOULD JUST ABOUT HAVE KICKED THE HORNET'S NEST OVER BY NOW."
LOOK AT THIS. IT'S NOT ATTACKING. IT KNOWS US. WE HAVE PEACE.
THIS CAN BE THE FUTURE. WE CAN HAVE A FUTURE.
THIS IS WHAT HOPE LOOKS LIKE.
NO.

EVEN IF YOU WERE RIGHT, WE ACT LIKE THIS, WE DON'T DESERVE TO SURVIVE. AND YOU DO THIS, I SHOOT YOU SECOND.
SURVIVAL ISN'T ABOUT BEING PURE. IT'S NOT THE JUST WHO SURVIVE.
WE DO WHAT WE HAVE TO. AND RAVEN...
...SURVIVAL COMES TO THOSE WHO DO.
I'M SORRY.
I'M NOT.
SHIT.

MOLLY...
I KEEP MY PROMISES, CAM.
NO!
NO.
GO!
HAVE TO GO, BABY, HAVE TO GO.
AND WE DID.
NO.
AGAIN, NOT EASY.

FOR ANYONE.
THIS?
NO NO NO NO.
THIS WAS CAMERON'S GREATEST FEAR.
YES.
THIS...

...WAS THE DEATH OF HOPE.
NO.
NO...
DO YOU HAVE A PLAN?
NO.

I MEAN, NOT THE DEATH OF HOPE, THANK GOD.
BE HARD TO TELL THIS STORY IF IT WAS.
FIGHT UNTIL ALL OF THEM ARE DEAD.
OR WE ARE.
YOU'RE RIGHT, THAT ISN'T A PLAN.
OH SHIT.

NO.
WE NEED TO GET OUT.
YES.
IT DIDN'T HAVE TO BE THIS WAY.
WE COULD HAVE HAD A FUTURE.

I HAVE A PLAN.
SHIT.
SOMEONE ELSE HAS THE SAME PLAN.

IT DIDN'T HAVE TO BE THIS WAY.
WITH WHAT HAPPENED AFTER, I WONDER IF IT COULD HAVE BEEN DIFFERENT.
THAT'S OUR RIDE.
GO.
BUT WHAT HAPPENED HAPPENED.
AND THEY NEEDED TO GET THE HELL OUT OF SANCTUARY.
AND HERE...
...WE...

...GO!
OF COURSE...

...THERE WERE PROBLEMS.
SEVERAL ACTUALLY.
WE NEED TO FIND THEM.
I DON'T SEE THEM.
WE CAN'T STOP. NOT WHILE THEY'RE STILL COMING.
BUT DON'T WORRY. I KEEP MY PROMISES.
"WE'LL FIND THEM."

SPLURP
YOU SAID...
YOU SAID WE WOULD BE SAFE. YOU SHOWED US. YOU...

YES, I DID.
IT APPEARS I WAS MISTAKEN.

NO.
BUT THERE'S ONE THING TO REMEMBER.
I AM THE ONE.
IN THIS WORLD...
I AM THE MESSAGE.
...THINGS CAN ALWAYS GET WORSE.

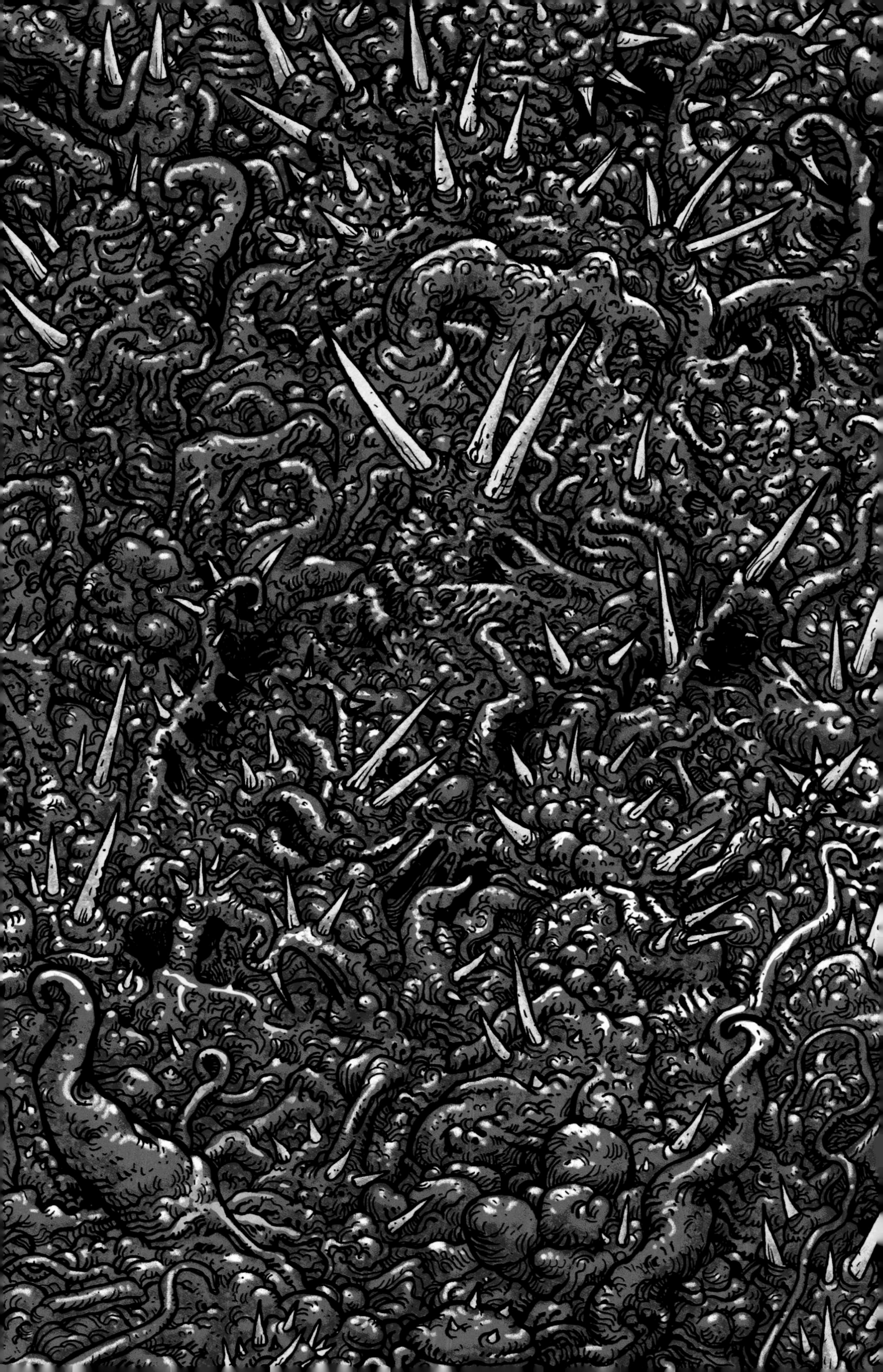

STORIES FROM THE SPREAD

FOOD CHAIN
script by JAMES MADDOX
art by DAVID STOLL
colors by NICK WENTLAND

NO SLEEP
script by KING EDDIE
art by ROSS TAYLOR

SKINS
script by AARON GILLESPIE
art by BALDEMAR RIVAS
letters by CRANK!

GLORY DAYS
script by AARON GILLESPIE
art & letters by SCOTT DRUMMOND

THE FOOD CHAIN
WRITTEN BY JAMES MADDOX
ILLUSTRATED BY DAVID STOLL
COLORS BY NICK WENTLAND
SPECIAL THANKS TO MICHAEL ADAMS FOR CHARACTER CONCEPTS
YOU CHECK OVER THERE?
OF COURSE I DID.
DAMN... DID SCAVENGERS NAB EVERY MORSEL IN THIS FROST-COVERED SHITSCAPE?
WELL, LOOKIE WHAT WE HAVE HERE.
SEEMS DINNER'S COMING TO US FOR A CHANGE.
JUST HOLD STILL, LITTLE BUDDY.
THIS'LL BE OVER IN A--
THUNK
DAMMIT!
DON'T LET IT GET AWAY!

IT DIDN'T JUST DISAPPEAR. IT COULDN'T HAVE.
KEEP LOOKING FOR TRACKS.
COULD FUCKIN' TASTE THAT CRITTER.
PAT, YOU HEAR A NOISE?
CREEAK
WHAT'S THIS HAPPY CRAP?
RRRRRR
RUN!
COME ON! COME ON!
ROAR

SHE'S LIT! READY WITH THAT BOW?
YES! THROW IT, ALREADY!
GOOD, JUST DON'T MISS THIS TIME.
BOOOSH
FLIPP
HOLE-EE SHIT, WE JUST NIXED US A GODDAM SPREAD-BEAR!
SUPPOSE WE COULD EAT WHAT'S LEFT?
YOU KIDDING? AFTER ALL THAT, I'M GOING VEGAN.
WITH VEGGIES IN SUCH GRAND SUPPLY? GOOD LUCK WITH THAT, DUM-DUM.

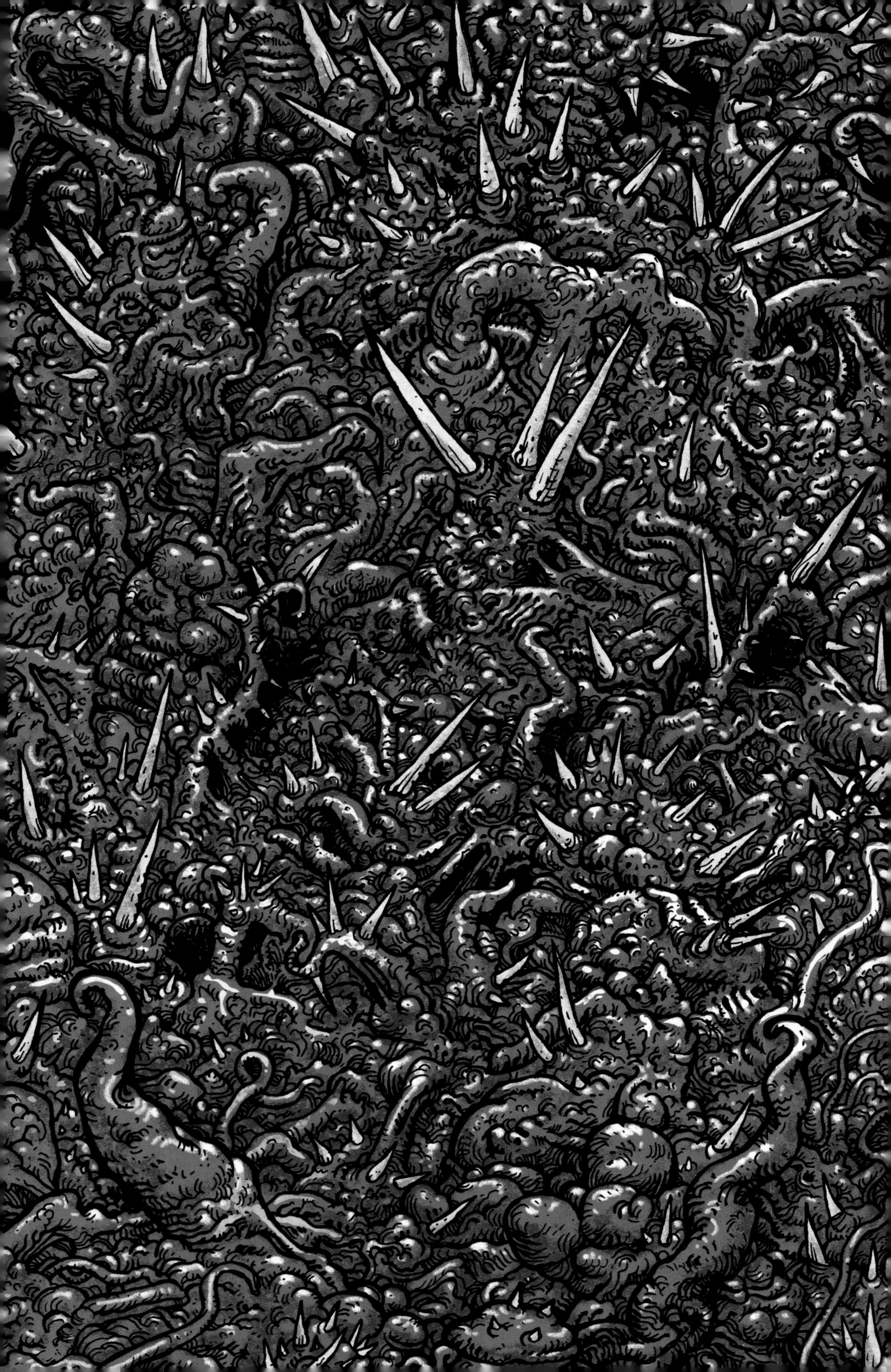

NO SLEEP
SCRIPT & LETTERS: KING EDDIE
ART: ROSS TAYLOR
SLEEP.
IT WAS NEVER VERY EASY FOR NO, LOOKING AFTER ME. BUT THAT FIRST NIGHT WAS ESPECIALLY TERRIBLE.
HE'D MET HIS MOST FORMIDABLE OPPONENT...
...AN EXHAUSTED BABY WHO REFUSED TO SLEEP.
STOP!
WE OFTEN HEARD THINGS AT NIGHT. AND SOMETIMES IT WAS JUST NOISE.
POP
CRACK
SOMETIMES IT WAS RAIDERS.
THWOOSH
SOMETIMES THOUGH, IT WAS MUCH WORSE.

THAT NIGHT TURNED OUT TO BE ONE OF THOSE "MUCH WORSE" SITUATIONS.
THE SPREAD HAD A WAY OF MAKING SURE THINGS WERE NEVER AS THEY APPEARED ON THE SURFACE.
SPLURT
THWMP

NO!
AH
AH
CHOO
HISSSSSS
NO WAS COMING TO UNDERSTAND THAT I TOO HAD THAT ABILITY

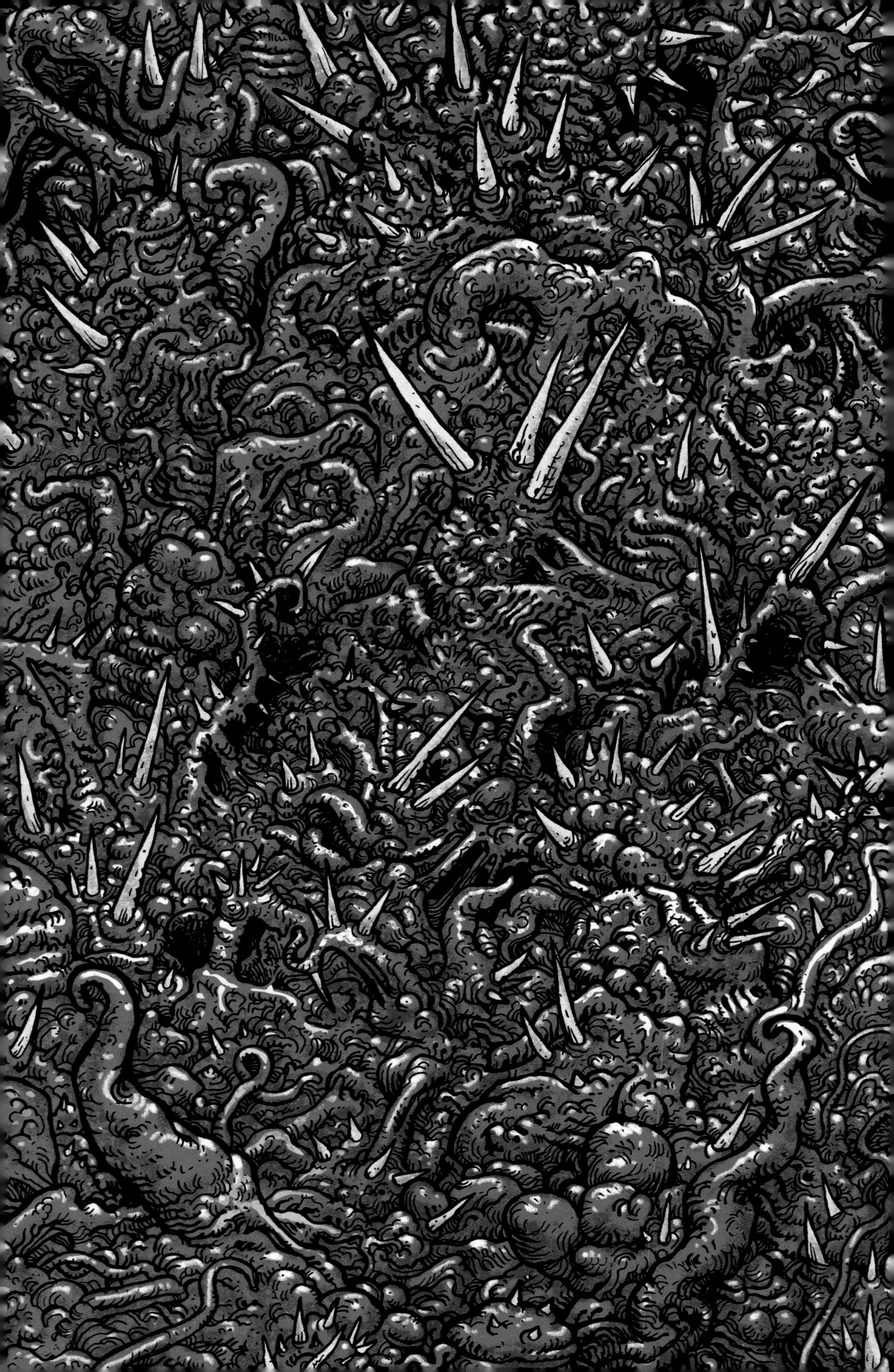

People used to laugh at the way I live. Called me **old-fashioned**. Said I was some kind of relic.
But they ain't laughing **now**, are they?
See, I know how to get the land to give up her goods. How to get the most out of the animals roaming all around.
When you show reverence to your prey, they give you more than just sustenance. They give you their power. Their **essence**.
I don their skin for more than just warmth. I meld with their **spirit**.
I **become** them.
I gain their keen senses.
RRRRRR
Their quick reflexes...

...and their brutal efficiency.
SHUNK
But most importantly, my prey gives me their power of survival.
GRRRRRRR
But now my prey betrays me.

YAAAUGH!
SHRIIID

My location is compromised.
I have to move.
With my old skin shed, time to do what I have always done.
Harvest a **new** one.
LET'S SEE WHAT I AM TO BECOME THIS TI--
...
OH, COME ON.

Thing about a new skin is, sometimes it fits like a glove.
And sometimes...
...well...
CRNCH
...sometimes it takes a while to grow into.
WORDS:
AARON GILLESPIE
ART:
BALDEMAR RIVAS
LETTERS:
CRANK!
The End

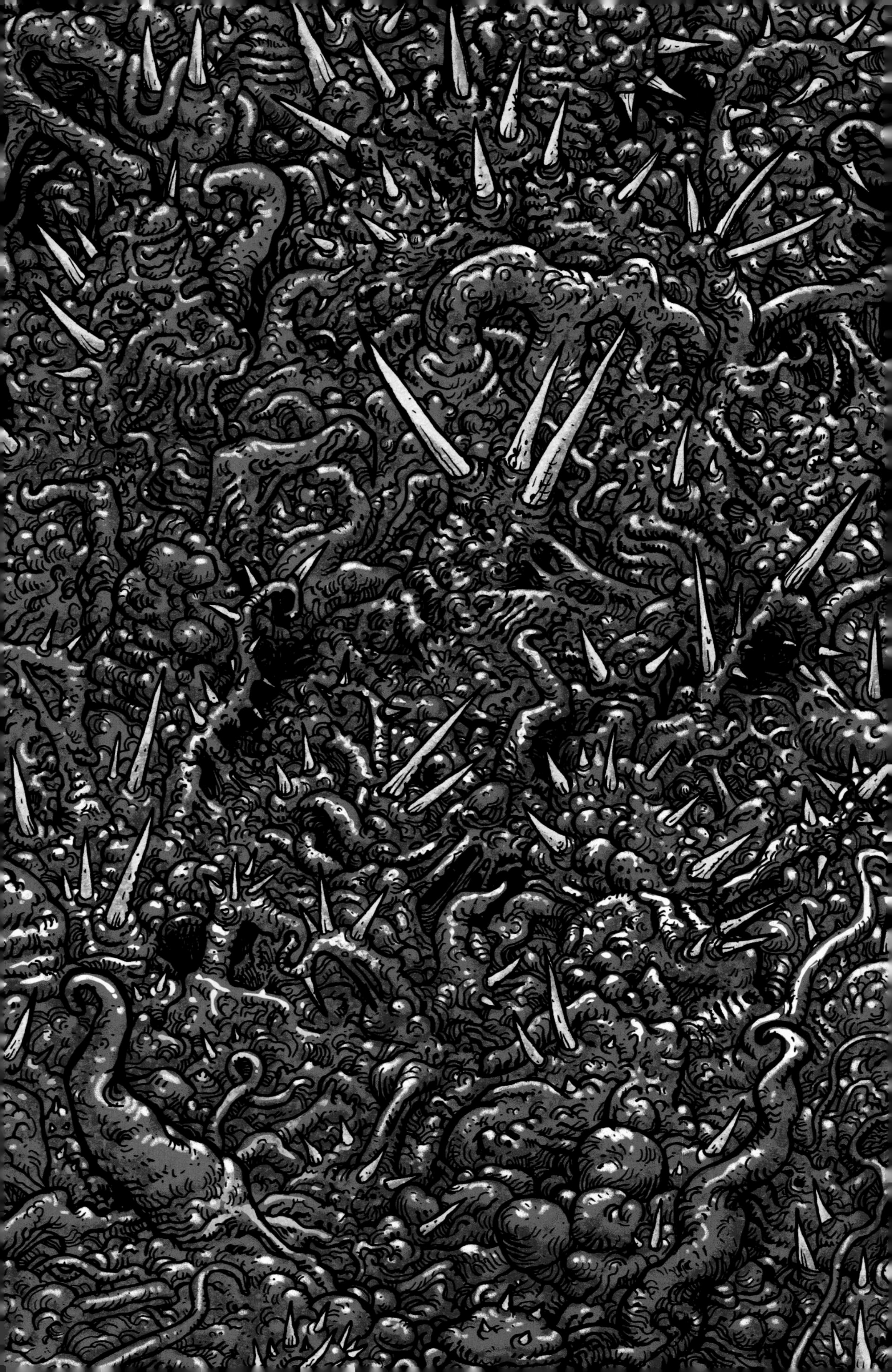

THIS IS IT.
THIS IS MY HAPPY ENDING.
OVER TWO DECADES OF ENDLESS DAYS AND NIGHTS ON THE ROAD. THE MENTAL FATIGUE AND THE PHYSICAL ABUSE.
BUT IT ALL PAID OFF.
MY NAME ON THE LIPS OF EVERY FAN IN PACKED-TO-CAPACITY ARENAS. FANS THAT STOOD IN LINE ALL AFTERNOON JUST TO GET A GLIMPSE OF ME. LIKE I WAS SOME KIND OF GOD.
SOMEONE TO WORSHIP.
CHAMPION
A HERO TO PEOPLE ALL AROUND THE WORLD.
BEST OF ALL TIME?
AND I GOT SOMETHING RARE IN THIS BUSINESS. I GOT TO GO OUT ON TOP AND STAY THERE.
MAX BRODY
AH, WHO AM I KIDDING?
ANYONE FOLLOWS WRESTLING KNOWS THE TRUTH.
HAPPY ENDINGS ARE BULLSHIT.
GLORY DAYS
SCRIPT: AARON GILLESPIE
ART & LETTERS: SCOTT DRUMMOND

A'WRIGHT, BIG DADDY, LISTEN UP...
'CUZ I AIN'T REPEATING MYSELF.
I BEEN AT THIS GAME A LONG DAMN TIME. FACED DOWN A LOT GOOD MEN.
TITO CRANE, BRIAN ASH, THE MAD HILLBILLY CLEM PUTNEY...
WAS A TIME I'D'VE TOLD YOU THOSE WERE MY TOUGHEST OPPONENTS.
BUT NOT NO MORE.
AT SOME POINT, MY BIGGEST ENEMY BECAME THE SAD SON OF A BITCH IN THIS MIRROR.
CONSTANTLY REMINDING ME OF ALL THE THINGS I DONE WRONG. THINGS I SHOULD HAVE DONE DIFFERENTLY. THINGS I FAILED TO DO AT ALL.
MOST DAYS, IT'S MORE'N A MAN CAN TAKE.
BUT THEN CAME THE DAY YOU FOUND ME, BIG DADDY.
YOU SAW DEEP INSIDE ME. PAST ALL THE PAIN AND THE BULLSHIT. ALL THE WAY DOWN TO THE *TRUTH.*
YOU KNEW THERE WAS STILL SOME GRIT LEFT IN THIS BROKEN-DOWN OLD MAN!
YOU ISSUED THE CHALLENGE AND I ACCEPT!
SO NOW IT'S TIME TO SHOW THE WORLD WHAT YOU SAW, BIG DADDY!
WRESTLING'S ABOUT ONE THING: FIGHTING THE GOOD FIGHT!
AND AIN'T NO ONE DOES THAT BETTER THAN...
COMIN'
FOR YA!
MAX GODDAMN BRODY!

I WAS WRONG.
ALRIGHT, BIG DADDY...
MY STORY *CAN* HAVE A HAPPY ENDING.
LET'S DO THIS!
I JUST HAD TO KNOW THE RIGHT TIME TO *FADE TO BLACK!*

INTERLOCKING VARIANT COVERS FROM SPREAD #14-17

ART BY KYLE STRAHM

No. 00012
Ages 18 and up
SPREAD™
103 1 KEY
$3.50
MOLLY™
WITH
BABY HOPE
AND
SPREAD FLYER
image®
Meets or exceeds all safety requirements of Product Standard JJKSFS
Jordan - Hickman - Sobreiro
Cover by Michael Adams and Kyle Strahm

SPREAD
+SOBREIRO

Jordan - Sobreiro
Cover by Michael Adams and Kyle Strahm

FELIPE SOBREIRO

“Sketch Cover” KYLE STRAHM

JUSTIN JORDAN • KYLE STRAHM • FELIPE SOBREIRO
image
ISSUE 6
SPREAD
Strahm '16 AFTER TODD
KYLE STRAHM

PIN-UPS

KELLY WILLIAMS

BALDEMAR RIVAS

BALDEMAR
RIVAS

DOUG FIRMINO

CAMILA TORRANO

Cosplay by YAMAL DURYEA

INTRODUCING THE
SPREAD™
T-SHIRT STORE AT THREADLESS!
spread's Artist Shop | Featuring custom t-shirts, prints, and more - Mozilla Firefox
File Edit View History Bookmarks Tools Help
https://spread.threadless.com
Search
spread's Artist Shop | Featuring custo...
Menu
SPREAD
0
SPREAD
SPREAD
http://spread.threadless.com/
GET COVERED IN IT.

JUSTIN JORDAN

Justin Jordan lives in the wilds of Pennsylvania and writes comics. Lots of comics. Most notably the *Luther Strode* saga and *Dead Body Road* for Image.

Twitter: @Justin_Jordan
Email: JustinJordan@gmail.com
Facebook: www.facebook.com/JustinJordanComics/

KYLE STRAHM

Kyle Strahm lives and works in a house in Kansas City, Missouri where he watches tv shows from back when they did it right and he rearranges old toys like a crazy person. You might have seen his work published by Marvel, DC, Dark Horse, IDW, Todd McFarlane Productions and various others.

Website: www.kylestrahm.com
Instagram: kylestrahm_art
Twitter: @kstrahm
Facebook: www.facebook.com/krstrahm

JOHN BIVENS

John draws stuff. Examples of this include the book you are holding now, *Dark Engine* (Image Comics), *Old Wounds* (Pop Goes the Icon), and multiple anthologies and such. He lives in Minneapolis.

Website: www.john-bivens.com
Instagram: bivensjohn
Twitter: @John_Bivens
Facebook: www.facebook.com/ArtOfJohnThomasBivens
Tumblr: johnbivens.tumblr.com

FELIPE SOBREIRO

Felipe Sobreiro is an artist and colorist from Brazil. His work has been published, among others, by Image, Marvel, DC, BOOM! Studios and Dark Horse. He's the colorist of the *Luther Strode* saga.

Website: www.sobreiro.com
Instagram: sobreiro
Twitter: @therealsobreiro
Facebook: www.facebook.com/fsobreiro

CRANK!

Crank! letters a bunch of books put out by Image, Dark Horse and Oni Press. He also has a podcast with Mike Norton (www.crankcast.net) and he makes music (www.sonomorti.bandcamp.com).

Twitter: @ccrank

SEBASTIAN GIRNER

Sebastian Girner is a freelance editor and writer who has helped creatively guide and produce comics for such publishers as Marvel Entertainment, Image Comics, VIZ Media and Random House. He lives and works in Brooklyn.

Website: www.sebastiangirner.com
Twitter: @SGirner

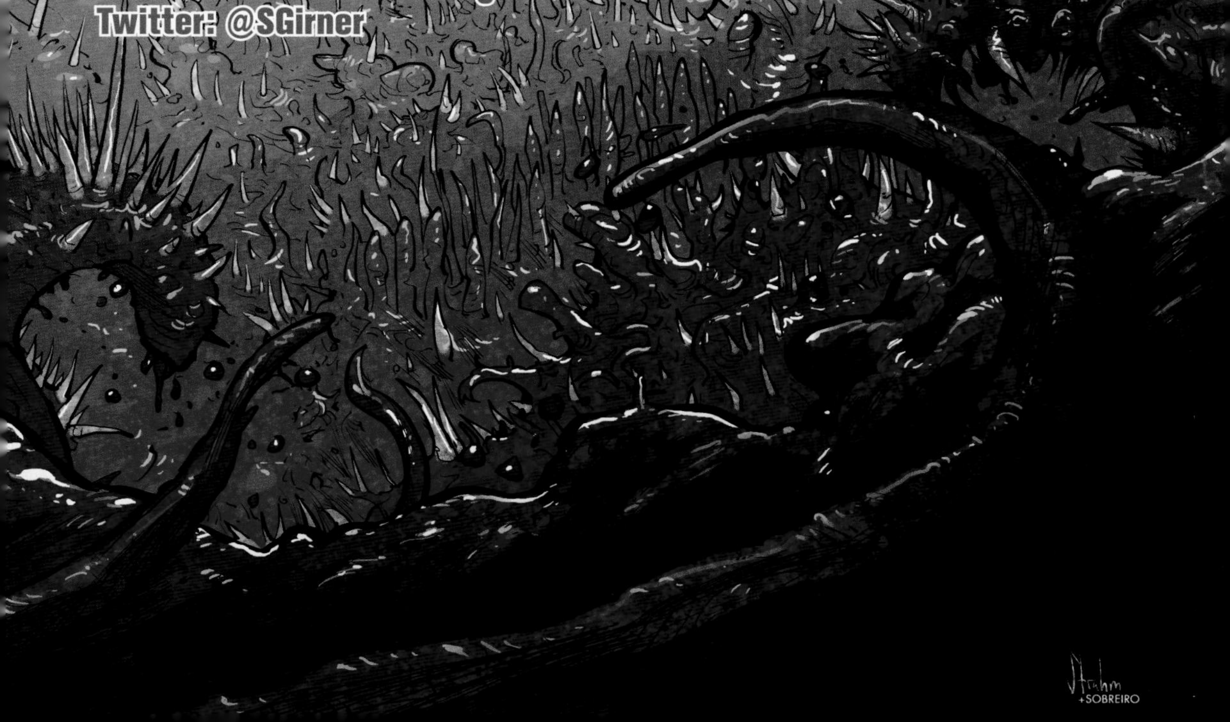

SPREAD
WILL RETURN WITH VOLUME FOUR.

Cranberry Salad Deluxe

Oyster Stew

Baked Stuffed Eggplant

Appetizer tray: Crabmeat canapés

CRAB MEAT CANAPÉS

1	**cup fresh lump crab meat, picked over well to remove any shell bits**
1/4	**cup mayonnaise**
1	**tablespoon chopped parsley**
1	**tablespoon chopped chives**
1	**teaspoon lemon juice**
1	**teaspoon Worcestershire sauce**
	Tabasco pepper sauce to taste
	Freshly ground pepper to taste
	Toast rounds

Combine the crab meat with the mayonnaise, herbs and seasonings. Spread on rounds of toast. Broil until browned. Makes 16 canapes.

HOT CLAM DIP

1	**8 ounce can minced clams**
2	**tablespoons butter or margarine**
2	**tablespoons minced onion**
2	**tablespoons catsup**
	Few drops hot pepper sauce
1	**cup diced sharp Cheddar cheese**
2	**tablespoons chopped ripe olives**
1	**teaspoon Worcestershire sauce**

Drain clams, reserving 1 tablespoon liquid. Melt butter in skillet, add onion and cook until tender but not brown. Add clams, 1 tablespoon reserved liquid, catsup, hot pepper sauce, cheese, olives and Worcestershire sauce. Cook until cheese is melted. Serve in a chafing dish with tortilla chips. Serves 4 - 6.

CLAMS CASINO

12 - 24 clams, depending on size
1/4 cup butter at room temperature
1 tablespoon finely minced pimiento
1 tablespoon finely minced green pepper
1 tablespoon finely minced celery
1/4 cup fine bread crumbs
1 teaspoon anchovy paste
6 slices bacon

Heat oven to 425 degrees. Scrub clams thoroughly and open with a strong knife. Cut clam away from shell but leave in half shell. Combine butter, pimiento, green pepper, celery, bread crumbs and anchovy paste. Work mixture to a paste and spread onto opened clams. Cut bacon into pieces large enough to cover each clam and place on top of mixture. Bake 8 to 10 minutes or until bacon is done.

CRAB-STUFFED MUSHROOMS

12 large or 24 medium sized mushrooms
5 tablespoons butter
2 tablespoons minced green onion
1 teaspoon lemon juice
1 cup flaked, cooked crab meat
1/2 cup soft bread crumbs
1 egg, lightly beaten
1/2 teaspoon dill weed
3/4 cup shredded Jack cheese
1/4 cup dry white wine
Lemon wedges

Wipe mushrooms with a damp cloth; remove the stems and finely chop them. Saute mushroom stems and onion in 2 tablespoons of the butter until onion is limp. Remove from heat and stir in lemon juice, crab, bread crumbs, egg, dill weed, and 1/4 cup of the cheese.

Melt remaining 3 tablespoons butter in a 9 by 13 inch baking pan. Turn mushroom caps in the butter to coat. Spoon about 2 tablespoons filling in each large cap (1 tablespoon in medium cap). Place mushrooms, filled side up in pan. Before baking, sprinkle mushrooms with remaining cheese and pour wine into pan. Bake in a 400 degree oven for 15 to 20 minutes. Serve hot with lemon wedges. Serves 6.

CHEESE PUFFS

1 cup grated Cheddar cheese
1 cup chopped onion
1 cup mayonnaise
Bread, cut into rounds

Mix ingredients together and spread on bread rounds. Bake in 350 degree oven until tops are bubbly and lightly browned, about 15 minutes. Serves 6-8

CRISP PARMESAN STRIPS

12 slices white bread
1 cup melted butter
$1^{1/2}$ cups grated Parmesan cheese
Paprika

Trim crusts from bread; cut each slice in 4 strips. Dip bread in butter, then into cheese. Place strips 1/2 inch apart on cookie sheet. Bake at 400 degrees for 8-10 minutes. Transfer to wire rack; sprinkle with paprika. Makes 48.

Clams Casino

BAKED STUFFED CLAMS

12 medium-size cherrystone clams, well scrubbed
2 tablespoons water
Rock salt (optional)
2 tablespoons butter
2 shallots, finely chopped
2 cloves garlic, finely chopped
2 cups soft bread crumbs
1/4 cup finely chopped celery
2 tablespoons chopped parsley
1/2 teaspoon dry basil
1/2 teaspoon oregano
2 tablespoons freshly grated Parmesan cheese
1 tablespoon olive oil
1 tablespoon dry white wine
Freshly ground black pepper
8 slices bacon, cut into thirds

Place the clams and water in a pan, cover and steam until clams open. Reserve the liquid, remove the clams from the shells and chop finely. Wash the shells and place on rock salt in shallow baking pan. Melt butter in a skillet and saute the shallots and garlic until just tender. Add the bread crumbs, celery, parsley, basil, oregano, cheese, oil, wine and pepper. Mix well. Stir in enough of reserved liquid to moisten crumbs but not make it soggy. Distribute the chopped clams among the shells, top with bread crumb mixture and a piece of the bacon. Bake in preheated 350 degree oven for 10 minutes and then broil until browned. Serves 4.

TORTILLA ROLL-UPS

1 cup sour cream
1 8 ounce package cream cheese
1 cup shredded Cheddar cheese
1 4 ounce can chopped green chilies
1 4 ounce can chopped black olives
1 cup chopped green onion

Mix together and spread on 5 flour tortillas. Roll up. Refrigerate, slice and serve after thoroughly chilled. Makes 20.

SALMON BALL

1 large can salmon (red)
1 8 ounce package cream cheese
2 teaspoons diced onion
1 teaspoon horseradish
2 tablespoons lemon juice
Dash of Tabasco pepper sauce
1/2 cup chopped pecans
1/4 cup minced parsley

Mix first 6 ingredients together and shape into ball. Roll in pecans and parsley. Serve with crackers.

Clam Chowder

NEW ENGLAND CLAM CHOWDER

2	**pounds clams (1 lb. shelled or canned clams)**
3	**oz. rindless bacon, diced**
1	**medium onion, finely diced**
1	**tablespoon flour**
6	**medium potatoes, peeled and cubed**
4	**cups milk**
1	**cup light cream**
	Chopped parsley (optional)

Saute bacon until fat is rendered. Remove bacon and set aside. Add onions to pan and cook until softened. Add the potatoes, salt, pepper, milk and reserved clam juice. Cover and boil twelve minutes or until potatoes are tender. Add the clams, cream, parsley and bacon and heat through. Do not boil. Serves 6.

CRANBERRY WALDORF MOLD

1	**12 ounce package fresh cranberries**
2/3	**cup sugar**
1	**envelope unflavored gelatin**
1	**cup fresh orange juice**
1	**cup chopped apple**
1/2	**cup chopped celery**
1/2	**cup chopped pecans or walnuts**

Wash and drain cranberries. In food processor, finely chop cranberries. In large bowl, combine cranberries and sugar; let stand 15 minutes, stirring occasionally. Sprinkle gelatin over orange juice in a small saucepan. Stir over medium heat until gelatin is completely dissolved, about 1 minute. Add gelatin mixture, apples, celery and nuts to cranberries. Mix well. Turn into oiled 1 quart mold. Refrigerate until firm. Serves 8.

Cranberry Salad

CRANBERRY SALAD DELUXE

1	**8 ounce package cream cheese, softened**
2	**tablespoons mayonnaise**
2	**tablespoons sugar**
1	**16 ounce can whole berry cranberry sauce**
1	**cup crushed pineapple with juice**
3/4	**cup chopped pecans**
1	**cup heavy cream, whipped**

Mix together the cream cheese, mayonnaise and sugar. Stir in the cranberry sauce, pineapple and pecans. Fold in whipped cream. Pour into 8 by 8 inch pan. Freeze until firm. Let thaw a few minutes before serving. Serves 10-12.

COLE SLAW

4	**cups finely shredded cabbage**
1/4	**cup sour cream**
1/4	**cup vinegar**
3	**tablespoons sugar**
1	**teaspoon salt**
1/8	**teaspoon dry mustard**

Mix together the sugar, salt, mustard, vinegar and sour cream. Pour over cabbage and mix well. Grated carrot or thinly sliced green pepper may be added. Serves 6.

OYSTER STEW

3	**dozen oysters with liquid**
2	**tablespoons butter**
1	**tablespoon flour**
2	**tablespoons chopped green onions**
2	**cups half and half (milk/cream)**
1	**teaspoon butter**
1/4	**teaspoon salt**
1	**dash Tabasco pepper sauce**

Heat oysters in liquid until their edges curl, then set aside to keep warm. Melt butter in a saucepan, blend in flour until smooth, stir in chopped green onions and simmer a few minutes. Pour into a blender with oyster liquid and one dozen of the oysters. Blend first on low, then high for about a minute. While blending, add cream (at room temperature). Melt one teaspoon of butter in a double boiler, add oyster mixture and stir until well heated and thickened. Season to taste. Add remaining oysters, or place six oysters in each warmed soup bowl and pour stew over them. Garnish with paprika. Serves 4.

CRAB CAKES

1	**pound crab meat**
1	**tablespoon mayonnaise**
1	**egg, beaten**
	Salt and pepper to taste
	Worcestershire sauce to taste
	French bread crumbs
4 - 6	**tablespoons butter**

Mix crab meat, mayonnaise, egg, salt, pepper and Worcestershire sauce; form into cakes. (The smaller you make the patties, the better they hold together.) Dip both sides of each cake in bread crumbs. Melt butter in a skillet. Cook crab cakes in butter over moderate heat until heated through and lightly browned. Serves 2 to 4.

LOBSTER BISQUE

1	**1 1/2 - 2 pound live lobster**
6	**tablespoons butter**
1/4	**cup finely diced carrot**
1	**small onion, diced**
	Bay leaf
	Pinch of thyme
3-4	**parsley sprigs**
3	**tablespoons cognac or brandy**
1/2	**cup dry white wine**
1/2	**cup fish stock**
1	**tablespoon Madeira wine**
1/4	**cup flour**
3	**cups milk**
3	**tablespoons cream**
1	**tablespoon tomato paste**

Split and clean lobster. Crack the claws and cut body into three or 4 pieces. Melt 2 tablespoons butter in skillet and saute the carrot and onions until softened. Add the bay leaf, thyme, parsley and lobster. Cook about 5 minutes. Add 2 tablespoons cognac and ignite. Add the wine and stock and simmer 20 minutes. Remove the lobster, cool and remove meat from shell. Dice, add the Madeira and set aside. Save the shell and broth. Melt the remaining butter in a saucepan, add the flour and stir. In the meantime, heat the milk to boiling. Add to flour mixture, stirring constantly.. Crush the lobster shell and add to the sauce. Add the reserved broth with the vegetables and simmer, covered for about 1 hour. Strain through a fine sieve. Bring sauce to a boil, add the cream and tomato paste. Add the reserved lobster meat, correct the seasonings and add the remaining cognac. Serves 4-5

SCAMPI

6	**tablespoons butter**
1/4	**cup olive oil**
2	**tablespoons parsley, minced**
2	**garlic cloves, minced**
1/2	**teaspoon salt**
2	**tablespoons lemon juice**
1	**pound large shrimp**
1 lb.	**steamed fresh spinach**

Preheat oven to 450 degrees. Melt the butter and add the olive oil, parsley, garlic, salt and lemon juice. Mix well. Shell and devein the shrimp, leaving the tails attached. Split down the inside lengthwise, being careful not to cut through the shrimp. Spread open to simulate butterflies. Place in a shallow baking pan, tail end up. Pour sauce over all. Bake for 5 minutes. Place under broiler for 5 minutes longer to brown. Serve over spinach. Serves 4.

Scampi

Baked Beans

BAKED BEANS

4	**cups navy beans**
3	**teaspoons salt**
1	**onion, minced**
1/2	**cup molasses**
2	**teaspoons mustard**
1/4	**teaspoon ginger**
1/2	**cup catsup**
1/2	**pound salt pork**

Soak beans overnight in cold water. Drain and add 2-1/2 quarts fresh water and minced onion. Cook slowly until skins burst. Drain and save liquid. Mix molasses, seasonings and catsup. Add 2 cups of liquid from the beans and the salt pork. Bake at 325 degrees in bean pot or deep dish for 1 to 2 hours. Serves 6.

CORN PUDDING

4	**ears fresh corn**
3	**beaten eggs**
1 1/2	**cup milk**
1	**teaspoon sugar**
	Dash salt
3	**tablespoons butter**

Cut corn from cobs and scrape ears. Combine all ingredients in buttered 1-1/2 quart casserole. Bake at 350 degrees for 45 minutes, or until set. Serves 6.

AU GRATIN POTATOES

6	**medium boiling or baking potatoes**
1/4	**cup butter**
1	**medium onion, chopped**
2	**tablespoons flour**
1	**teaspoon salt**
1/4	**teaspoon pepper**
2 1/2	**cups milk**
2	**cups shredded Cheddar cheese**
1/4	**cup fine dry bread crumbs**
	Paprika

Peel potatoes, boil until tender, approximately 20 minutes. Cool and dice into 1/2 in. cubes. Melt butter in medium saucepan and cook onion about 2 minutes. Stir in flour, salt and pepper. Cook stirring constantly for 1 minute. Stir in milk and 1 1/2 cups cheese. Stir and cook until smooth. Spread potatoes in ungreased 1 1/2 quart baking dish. Pour cheese sauce over potatoes. Bake uncovered for 1 hour in 350 degree oven. Mix remaining cheese and bread crumbs together and sprinkle over potatoes. Bake an additional 15 minutes until top is bubbly and browned slightly. Serves 6.

SUCCOTASH WITH HAM

2	**cups cooked, cubed ham**
2 1/2	**cups fresh lima beans**
2 1/2	**cups fresh corn**
1	**teaspoon salt**
3/4	**cup cream**

Cook lima beans until almost tender. About 10 minutes before serving, add corn, diced ham and salt. Heat through, add hot cream. Serves 8.

LIMA BEAN BAKE

2	**cups dried lima beans**
1 1/2	**teaspoons salt**
1/4	**cup unsulphured molasses**
1/4	**cup chili sauce**
1	**tablespoon cider vinegar**
	Cayenne pepper to taste
1/2	**teaspoon dry mustard**
1	**onion, chopped**
1	**cup cooked smoked ham, diced**
6	**slices bacon**

The day before, wash and pick over the beans. Cover with water and soak overnight. When ready to cook, add salt and simmer until beans are almost tender, about 45 minutes. Preheat oven to 325 degrees. Drain beans, reserving liquid. Combine the molasses, chili sauce, vinegar, cayenne and mustard. Mix with 1 cup of reserved liquid. Layer the beans with the onion and ham in a deep casserole. Pour the molasses mixture over all. Top with bacon. Bake, uncovered, 1-1/2 hours, adding more liquid during baking if necessary. Serves 6.

Lima Bean Bake

BAKED ACORN SQUASH

2 acorn squash
4 tablespoons maple syrup
4 tablespoons butter

Cut each squash lengthwise in half; remove seeds and fibers. Place squash, cut sides up, in ungreased pan. Spoon 1 tablespoon syrup and 1 tablespoon butter in each half. Bake approximately 45 minutes to 1 hour in 350 degree oven. Serves 4.

CUCUMBERS IN SOUR CREAM

1 large cucumber
1 cup sour cream
1 tablespoon chopped onion
3 tablespoons cider vinegar
1/4 teaspoon salt
1/8 teaspoon pepper

Peel the cucumber and run tines of fork lengthwise over cucumber and cut crosswise into thin slices. Combine the remaining ingredients and pour over sliced cucumber. Marinate thirty minutes at room temperature. Serves 4.

HARVARD BEETS

6 fresh beets, cooked, peeled, and diced or one can (1lb.) beets
1 tablespoon cornstarch
2 tablespoons water
3 tablespoons grated orange rind
1/4 teaspoon salt
3 tablespoons lemon juice
1/2 cup orange juice
1/4 cup butter

Blend cornstarch and water, add remaining ingredients, except beets. Bring to boiling point and cook, stirring constantly, until thick and smooth. Add beets and heat through. Serves 4.

BAKED STUFFED EGGPLANT

2 firm eggplants
1 tablespoon chopped parsley
1 cup cooked shrimp
1/4 cup bread crumbs
1 stick (1/2 cup) butter
4 tablespoons shallots, finely chopped
1 cup Parmesan cheese, finely grated
1 cup lump crab meat
Salt and pepper to taste

Cut eggplants in half and place in the oven at 375 degrees in a pan with a cup of water in the bottom to steam the eggplant. Cook until tender, about 30 minutes. Remove the pulp carefully with a spoon so that you do not break the skin. Brown shallots and parsley in butter over low heat. Add shrimp, crab meat and the eggplant pulp. Season with salt and pepper. Stir together and cook for 5 minutes. Fill the shells. Sprinkle cheese and bread crumbs over the top of each eggplant. Bake at 350 degrees until tops are browned. Serves 4.

Main Course

Lobster Newburg

Bouillabaisse

Yankee Pot Roast

Roast Turkey with Bread Stuffing

Steamed Clams

CLAM FRITTERS

12 clams, cooked, shelled, and drained (reserve broth)
$1^{1/2}$ cup flour
2 teaspoons baking powder
1/2 teaspoon salt
1/4 teaspoon pepper
1 egg, beaten
1/4 cup milk
1/4 cup clam broth
1 teaspoon minced parsley
1 tablespoon butter, melted and cooled
Fat for deep frying

Chop clams. Thoroughly mix dry ingredients. Combine egg, milk, clam broth, parsley, and butter. Pour over dry ingredients and beat well. Add the clams. Drop by tablespoons into hot fat (heated to 375 degrees). Brown on all sides, remove with slotted spoon and drain well. Serve hot, garnished with lemon wedges. Serves 4.

STEAMED CLAMS

1/4 cup butter
6 chopped shallots
1 clove garlic
1/4 cup dry white wine
1 bay leaf
36-48 scrubbed steamer clams

Saute the shallots and garlic in the butter until softened. Add the wine and bay leaf. Carefully add the clams and cook covered until clams open. Pour the clams, shells and all into heated bowls and serve garnished with chopped parsley. A crusty country loaf to accompany this is great for soaking up the broth. Serves 4-6.

HERB NUT-CRUSTED SALMON WITH HERB SAUCE

1 large or 2 small salmon fillets (at least 1 in. thick, 6 ounces per person)
1/2 cup finely chopped nuts
3 tablespoons soft butter
1/4 cup finely chopped herbs (tarragon, thyme, basil)

Mix together the nuts, butter and herbs and spread over top of salmon. Bake in preheated 350 degree oven and cook for approximately 20 minutes or until salmon is cooked through. Do not overcook.

In the meantime, make the Herb Sauce:

1/2 cup mixed finely chopped herbs (basil, thyme, tarragon)
3 tablespoons dry white wine
1 tablespoon finely chopped shallots
1 cup heavy cream
1 tablespoon lime juice
salt and pepper to taste

Mix together in saucepan the wine, herbs and shallots. Cook together approximately 13 minutes. Add cream and lime juice and cook another 10 minutes until somewhat reduced. Puree mixture in blender until smooth. Set aside and reheat before serving. Serves 4.

CODFISH CAKES

1/2 pound salt cod, soaked overnight
1 cup mashed potatoes
2 eggs
Pepper to taste

Cut cod into small pieces, cover with water and bring to a boil. Taste for saltiness. If excessively salty, discard the water and repeat until the water is almost fresh. Mix the fish, potatoes, eggs and pepper together. Form into 8 cakes and saute in plenty of hot butter until browned and cooked through. Serves 4.

BAKED STUFFED HADDOCK

1/2 cup chopped onion
1/4 cup chopped celery
1/2 cup chopped fresh mushrooms
3 tablespoons butter
2 cups soft bread crumbs
1 teaspoon salt
1/8 teaspoon pepper
Pinch of dried tarragon and rosemary
2 pounds haddock fillets
Lemon juice
3-4 sliced tomatoes

Saute the onion, celery and mushrooms in the butter. Remove from heat and stir in the bread crumbs, salt, pepper and herbs. Layer the fish in a greased baking dish. Top with lemon juice. Spread the stuffing over fish, top with sliced tomatoes and bake uncovered for 35-40 minutes or until fish flakes. Serve with boiled potatoes. Serves 6.

Baked Stuffed Haddock

BROILED HADDOCK WITH LEMON & HERBS

2 pounds haddock fillets
3 tablespoons lemon juice
Salt and pepper to taste
2 tablespoons butter
1/2 cup olive oil
1 1/2 teaspoons water
2 tablespoons fresh herbs, (parsley, thyme, tarragon)

Preheat broiler. Cut fish into serving pieces and place on oiled broiler pan. Brush with 1 tablespoon of the lemon juice and season with salt, pepper and herbs. Broil for about 8 minutes or until fish flakes. Combine the oil, herbs, water and salt to taste. Heat and stir until well blended. Pour over fish and serve. Serves 6.

FRIED CLAMS

24 clams, shucked and drained
1/2 cup milk
1 egg, separated
1 tablespoon butter
1/4 teaspoon salt
1/2 cup flour
Fat for deep frying

Beat the egg yolk with 1/4 cup milk. Stir in the butter, salt and flour and beat until smooth. Gradually beat in remaining milk. Beat the egg white until stiff. Fold into batter. Dip each clam into the batter and fry in hot fat (375 degrees). Serves 3-4.

BROILED GLOUCESTER SCROD

2 pounds scrod (young cod)
1/2 cup butter
1/4 cup chopped onion
1/4 cup lemon juice
Dash of Tabasco pepper sauce
2 cups bread crumbs
1/2 teaspoon dry mustard
1 tablespoon minced parsley
salt and pepper to taste

Wipe scrod with damp towel. In skillet, melt 1/3 butter. Saute onion in butter until it is tender and translucent. Add lemon juice and Tabasco. Combine bread crumbs with mustard, parsley, salt, and pepper. Mix bread crumbs with butter-lemon sauce. Lay scrod on foil-lined broiler rack. Dot with remaining butter. Salt and pepper to taste. Broil 5 minutes. Turn and top with crumbs. Broil approximately 5 minutes more or until cooked through. Garnish with parsley and lemon. Serves 4.

OYSTERS ON THE 1/2 SHELL

6 fresh shucked oysters per serving
Lemon wedges
Hot pepper sauce
Ground black pepper
Buttered toast points

To shuck oysters, insert strong knife into hinge side of shell and twist to open. Loosen each oyster from the deeper half shell but let it remain in the shell. Discard other half. Serve on a bed of cracked ice around a small bowl of hot pepper sauce. Sprinkle with coarse ground black pepper and a squeeze of lemon. Serve with toast points.

Oysters on the 1/2 Shell

BOILED MAINE LOBSTER

Use only live lobsters. Claws should be left pegged. Fill a large kettle 2/3 full of water. Add 1/4 cup salt. Cover and bring to boil. Plunge the lobsters into the water head first. Cover. Begin counting the cooking time when the water comes back to a boil. Cook 15-20 minutes for 1-2 pound lobsters. Do not overcook. Plunge cooked lobsters into cold water for 30 seconds to stop cooking. Twist off the large claws. Drain off liquid. Serve with lots of melted butter and lemon.

LOBSTER NEWBURG

4	**tablespoons butter**
2	**cups boiled, diced lobster meat**
1/4	**cup Madeira or dry sherry**
1/2	**teaspoon paprika**
1/8	**teaspoon ground nutmeg**
3	**egg yolks**
1	**cup cream**

In a double boiler, melt the butter. Add the lobster meat and cook about 2 minutes. Add the Madeira and spices. Beat together the egg yolks and cream and add to lobster mixture. Cook and stir constantly until thickened. Do not boil. Remove from heat and serve over hot buttered toast points. Serves 4.

LOBSTER ROLL

2	**cooked lobsters, about 1 1/2 lb. each**
2	**stalks celery**
1/2	**cup mayonnaise**
4	**hot dog rolls**
4	**tablespoons melted butter**

Remove the lobster meat from the tails and claws and cut into pieces. Combine the meat with the celery and mayonnaise, cover and chill for at least 30 minutes. Preheat broiler. Open the hot dog rolls and brush with the melted butter. Place the rolls, buttered side up, in a hot broiler and toast lightly. Line roll with lettuce. Fill each roll with the lobster mixture and serve immediately. Serves 4.

BROILED CAPE SCALLOPS

3	**pounds Cape scallops**
1/2	**pound butter**
	Juice of 1 lemon
1	**cup bread crumbs**
1	**tablespoon finely chopped parsley**
1/4	**teaspoon thyme**
	Salt and pepper to taste
	Paprika

Dry scallops with towel. Melt the butter in heavy casserole. Add lemon juice and scallops. Mix well until scallops are coated. Mix bread crumbs and seasonings. Spread crumbs on top . Broil until cooked through, about 10 minutes. Do not overcook. Serve with lemon wedges. Serves 6.

BOUILLABAISSE

2	**leeks, washed and sliced**
1	**onion sliced**
3	**tablespoons olive oil**
4	**garlic cloves**
3	**bay leaves**
2	**carrots, chopped**
6	**potatoes, cubed**
1/2	**teaspoon fennel seeds**
2	**teaspoons orange zest**
4	**sprigs parsley**
3	**cups fish stock**
3	**large ripe tomatoes**
	Juice of 1 lemon
3	**pounds assorted fish and shellfish (haddock, lobster, scallops, perch, shrimp, mussels)**
1	**cup chopped parsley**
3-4	**threads saffron**
	Salt to taste

Saute in a large soup pot the leeks and onion in the olive oil until tender. Add the garlic, bay leaves, carrots and black pepper and cook for 5 minutes. Add the potatoes, fennel, orange zest, thyme. Cook another 10 minutes. Add the stock, water, tomatoes and lemon juice. Continue cooking until potatoes and carrots are tender. Mix in the fish, saffron, and parsley and cook for 3-4 minutes. Add salt to taste. Serve in heated bowls with crusty French bread. Serves 6.

FISH CHOWDER

1	**pound salt cod (soaked overnight and rinsed several times until water is fresh)**
1	**pound fresh cod fillets**
1	**pound haddock fillets**
4	**tablespoons butter**
1	**onion, chopped**
3	**cups heavy cream**
3	**cups milk**
1	**teaspoon thyme, dried**
1/4	**pound bacon**
2	**cups potatoes, diced**
3	**tablespoons chopped parsley**
	Pepper

Cut fish into 1 inch pieces. Refrigerate while preparing chowder base. Saute the onions in the butter until soft. Add the cream, milk and thyme and simmer for 15 minutes. Meanwhile, dice the bacon and cook until crisp. Drain and set aside. Add the potatoes to the chowder and cook another 15 minutes until potatoes are tender. Add the fish and simmer for about 10 more minutes. Season to taste. Serve in warmed soup bowls and garnish with parsley and the browned bacon pieces.

NEW ENGLAND CLAMBAKE

Something of a cross between a picnic and a banquet, the clambake is a New England "original". It's the perfect way to combine a day of fun at the beach by preparing heaps of food for hungry people. The Indians invented it. When tribes moved from their winter quarters inland to their summer camps along the coast, the abundant shellfish, freshly caught, were cooked in steam pits while games were played on the shore. A clambake starts very early in the morning, First a hole is dug whose size depends on the number of people to be fed. It can be as much as 8 feet in length. This is lined with melon-shaped stones. The "bake" is allowed to burn until the stones are red-hot -- an hour or two, at least. Assistants rake off the embers and throw baskets of seaweed over the stones. Rockweed, with its rubbery air pockets is best. Next, cheesecloth bags filled with clams and lobsters are laid in. More seaweed is added. Potatoes in their jackets, corn with the silk removed but not the husks, small peeled onions, sausages -- whatever fancy dictates is included, each food in its own bag, layered in seaweed. This work must be done fast to capture the steam. Last, the mound of food receives its top blanket of seaweed followed by a tarpaulin secured with stones. That's all there is to it, except for the waiting while delicious aromas of steaming seafood seep into the air to tantalize guests. Someone can melt lots of butter. There should be plenty of hot rolls and cold drinks. It seems forever, but, finally, cautious testing by the bakemaster reveals that the potatoes and onions are tender so everything else must be cooked. Although uniformly flavored by seaweed, never will the taste of each food seem so distinctly delicious! Dessert is always fresh watermelon, cut to order.

Yankee Pot Roast

YANKEE POT ROAST

5 pounds lean, boneless chuck or 7- bone cut
1 quart water
1 tablespoon sugar
1 stalk celery
2 onions, sliced
1 tablespoon salt
2 teaspoons pepper
1/2 teaspoon curry powder
1/2 teaspoon cinnamon
1/2 teaspoon allspice
1 teaspoon dry mustard
$1^{1/2}$ carrots, per person
2 potatoes, per person

Combine water, sugar, celery, onions, salt, pepper and spices. Pour the mixture over the meat and allow it to stand overnight.. Remove the meat and sear on all sides. Pour liquid over the meat and cook in a 300 degree oven for 3-4 hours. During the last hour, add the carrots and potatoes, placing the carrots on top of the meat. Thicken the drippings with flour and milk, if desired.

BAKED WHOLE HAM

1 cured ham
1/4 cup brown sugar
Cloves

Bring ham to room temperature. Score top side of ham in criss-cross diamonds and stud with cloves. Cover with brown sugar and place, fat side up, in a roasting pan. Add a generous amount of water and cover roasting pan. Bake at 325 degrees, allowing 10 to 15 minutes per pound

Pork Chops and Rice Casserole

PORK CHOPS & RICE CASSEROLE

4 pork chops
2 tablespoons shortening
1 cup uncooked rice
1 16 ounce can tomatoes
1 onion, sliced
1 can beef consomme
1 teaspoon thyme
Salt and pepper

Brown pork chops in a small amount of shortening. Place uncooked rice in a greased 1-1/2 quart casserole and lay pork chops over rice. Add the other ingredients and cook at 350 degrees for l hour. Serves 4.

PORK LOIN ROAST WITH YAM-STUFFED APPLES

1 pork loin roast, about 6 pounds
Salt, pepper and sage
6-8 large tart baking apples
1 16 ounce can sweet potatoes
1/4 cup brown sugar
1 teaspoon salt
1/4 teaspoon cinnamon
1/2 cup almonds, slivered
1/4 cup butter, melted
1/4 cup maple syrup

Rub pork with 1/2 teaspoon salt per pound. Sprinkle with pepper and sage. Place roast, fat side up, on rack in an open pan. Do not add water. Roast uncovered at 300 degrees for 4 to 4-1/2 hours or until well done. Wash and core apples. Remove enough pulp to make core opening about 1-1/4" wide. Mash sweet potatoes. Combine with apple pulp, brown sugar, salt, cinnamon and one half of the almonds. Blend butter and syrup in saucepan and spoon a little of the syrup mixture into the apple cavities. Fill cavities with sweet potato mixture. Mound a spoonful on top of each apple. Stud stuffing with remaining almonds. Place apples around roast or in separate dish the last 1-1/2 hours of baking time. Baste apples occasionally with remaining syrup. When roast is done, arrange apples and roast on heated serving platter. Serves 6.

BAKED MACARONI & VERMONT CHEDDAR CHEESE

1/2 pound elbow macaroni
3 tablespoons butter
2 tablespoons flour
1/4 teaspoon dry mustard
1 teaspoon salt
1/4 teaspoon pepper
2 cups milk
1/2 pound Vermont Cheddar cheese, grated
1/2 cup bread crumbs
Paprika

Cook macaroni in 1 quart of boiling water until tender. Meanwhile, melt 2 tablespoons butter in a double boiler. Add flour and seasonings, stirring to keep smooth. Gradually add milk and cook over hot water until hot and thickened. Add cheese and cook until just melted. Combine macaroni and cheese sauce in a casserole dish. Scatter bread crumbs on top, dot with remaining butter and sprinkle with paprika. Bake in 350 degree oven for 20-25 minutes. Serves 4.

MAINE BEEF STEW WITH PARSLEY DUMPLINGS

$1^{1/2}$	**pounds beef chuck, trimmed and cut into into cubes**
3	**tablespoons flour**
1/2	**teaspoon salt**
1/2	**teaspoon paprika**
1/4	**cup salt pork drippings**
1	**cup chopped onion**
1	**quart beef stock**
1	**bay leaf**
1/4	**cup chopped parsley**
4	**potatoes, peeled and cubed**
3	**carrots, scraped and sliced**

Shake beef cubes in a bag with the flour, salt and paprika. In a large skillet, brown beef well on all sides in salt pork drippings. Add onion, stir and cook for 3 minutes. Add stock, bay leaf, and parsley. Bring to a boil, reduce heat and simmer, covered, until beef is tender, about 1 hour. Remove bay leaf. Add potatoes and carrots. Continue cooking for about 15 minutes.

Meanwhile, mix the dumplings.

$1^{1/2}$	**cups flour**
$3^{1/2}$	**teaspoons baking powder**
1/2	**teaspoons salt**
1/4	**cup finely chopped parsley**
1/4	**cup milk**

Stir together the dry ingredients. Stir in the parsley. Add the milk and mix with a fork until just blended. When vegetables are done, taste the gravy for seasoning. Drop the dumpling batter by tablespoons on the stew. Cover tightly and simmer for 12 minutes without lifting cover. Serves 6.

NEXT DAY CORNED BEEF HASH

3	**cups corned beef, finely chopped**
3	**cups potatoes, cooked and finely chopped**
1	**small onion, grated**
	Stock from cooking pot
	Salt and pepper to taste

Mix the corned beef and potatoes with the grated onion and enough of the stock left from cooking the corned beef to moisten slightly. Salt and pepper to taste. Form into thick patties and pan fry in hot fat until crusty and browned. Serve with poached eggs. Serves 4-6.

FILET DE BOEUF WITH BEARNAISE SAUCE

1	**whole beef tenderloin roast, 4 to 5 pounds**
2	**tablespoons butter**
1	**16 ounce can beef broth**

Rub beef with butter. Baste with broth. Bake at 350 degrees for 20 to 25 minutes (for rare) or 35 minutes (for medium). Serve on a platter with canned or cooked new potatoes browned in butter, warmed cherry tomatoes and fresh green beans. To serve, pool individual serving plates with a scoop of Bearnaise Sauce and slices of tenderloin. Surround with vegetables.

Corn Beef Hash

NEW ENGLAND BOILED DINNER

5	**pound corned brisket of beef**
8-9	**potatoes, peeled and halved**
6	**carrots, scraped and halved**
1	**rutabaga, sliced**
6	**whole small onions**
1	**large head cabbage, cut into wedges**
12	**small beets, cooked**

Put corned beef in large pot with enough water to cover meat. Bring to a boil, reduce heat and simmer for 3 hours. Add water as needed to keep meat covered. When meat is tender, remove and keep warm. Put potatoes, carrots, rutabaga, and onions into the pot and cook for 15 minutes. Add cabbage and cook another 10 minutes. Heat beets separately. Horseradish and mustard are traditionally served with this. Serves 6.

ROAST TURKEY WITH BREAD STUFFING

1	**14-16 pound cleaned turkey**
1/4	**cup butter**
1	**cup celery, finely chopped**
1	**cup onion, finely chopped**
2	**tablespoons chopped parsley**
1/2	**teaspoon thyme**
1	**tablespoon sage**
1	**teaspoon salt**
	Pepper
1 1/2	**pounds day-old bread, broken into small pieces.**
2	**eggs**
1 1/2	**cup chicken stock or water**

Melt butter in pan and saute onion, celery and parsley together. Add seasonings and mix well. Cool. Stir in the bread pieces. Combine the eggs and stock and gently stir into the bread mixture.

Fill the turkey cavity with the stuffing. Do not pack tightly. Put remaining stuffing into a greased casserole and refrigerate until last 45 minutes of turkey roasting time. Bake turkey, uncovered in large roasting pan, breast side up in 325 degree preheated oven about 20 minutes per pound. Baste frequently with pan drippings.

Breads & Desserts

Blueberry Coffee Cake

Boston Cream Pie

Popcorn With Maple Syrup

Corn Fritters

Blueberry Muffins

BLUEBERRY MUFFINS WITH STREUSEL TOPPING

2	**cups self-rising flour**
1/3	**cup sugar**
1	**egg, beaten**
3/4	**cup milk**
1/4	**cup vegetable oil**
1	**cup fresh or frozen blueberries**
1/4	**cup brown sugar, firmly packed**
2	**tablespoons self-rising flour**
1	**tablespoon butter**

Combine 2 cups flour, 1/3 cup sugar in a large bowl, mixing well. Reserve 2 tablespoons of the mixture and set aside. Make well in center of remaining flour. Combine egg, milk and oil. Add to dry ingredients, stirring just until moistened. Combine blueberries and reserved 2 tablespoons flour, tossing to coat. Stir blueberries into batter just until blended. Fill greased muffin pans 3/4 full. Combine brown sugar, 2 tablespoons flour and butter. Mix until crumbly. Sprinkle over batter in muffin pans. Bake in preheated 400 degree oven for 15-18 minutes.

Note: If frozen berries are used, rinse and drain thawed berries. Pat dry. Makes 1 dozen.

BLUEBERRY COFFEE CAKE

1	**cup butter**
1	**cup sugar**
2	**eggs**
3	**cups flour**
1	**cup sour cream**
1	**teaspoon baking soda**
1	**teaspoon baking powder**
1/2	**teaspoon salt**
1	**teaspoon vanilla**

Mix all together well and put half into a well-greased 9 x 13 inch baking pan. Spread 1 can of blueberry pie filling over this. Pour the rest of the batter over the blueberry filling. Sprinkle with the following mixture: 1/4 cup flour, 3 tablespoons butter and 1/4 cup sugar. Bake for 45 minutes in a preheated 375 degree oven.

PUMPKIN BREAD

Pumpkins were one of the first plentiful New England crops. Along with corn and fish, this sweet vegetable must have been the mainstay of many a Pilgrim diet, because this little verse originates in the 17th century.

'We have pumpkins at morning,
Pumpkins at noon.
If it weren't for the pumpkins,
We should be undone!"

4	**eggs**
3	**cups sifted flour**
2	**teaspoons baking powder**
2	**teaspoons baking soda**
1 1/2	**teaspoons cinnamon**
1/2	**teaspoon ginger**
1/2	**teaspoon nutmeg**
1	**teaspoon salt**
2	**cups sugar**
1/2	**cup vegetable oil**
2	**cups canned pureed pumpkin**
1	**cup raisins**

Sift together the flour, baking soda, baking powder, spices and salt 2 times. Butter 2 loaf pans. Line the buttered pans with paper cut to fit. Mix oil and sugar in a large bowl. Add eggs one at a time, beating after each until mixture is light. Add flour alternately with pumpkin, beating well after each. Stir in raisins. Pour into pans. Bake in preheated 350 degree oven for 1 hour or until toothpick when inserted into center comes out clean. Makes 2 loaves

CORNBREAD

1 1/2	**cups yellow cornmeal**
1	**cup all-purpose flour, sifted**
1	**tablespoon baking powder**
1 1/4	**teaspoons salt**
3/4	**cup (1 and 1/2 sticks) unsalted butter, melted and cooled**
2	**large eggs, lightly beaten**
1 1/2	**cups milk**

Preheat oven to 375 degrees. Butter a 9 inch square pan. In a mixing bowl, sift together the cornmeal, flour, baking powder and salt. Add the butter, eggs and milk and stir until just combined. Pour into pan and bake about 40 minutes; or divide mix into corn stick mold pan and bake 20 minutes. Or double the recipe, pour into a greased heavy cast iron skillet that has been preheated. Bake for 25 to 30 minutes. Yields 6-9 servings.

BROWN BREAD

Steamed bread was popularized by New Englanders who didn't have ovens. The open hearth might accommodate only one kettle, which was always in use, sometimes to cook the evening stew. Sometimes it was being used for heating water for dishwashing. The brown bread could be steamed right in the kettle without disturbing its contents.

1	**cup milk**
1	**teaspoon vinegar**
1/2	**cup cornmeal**
1/2	**cup rye flour**
1/2	**cup whole wheat flour**
1/2	**teaspoon salt**
1/4	**teaspoon baking soda**
1/4	**cup molasses**
1/3	**cup raisins**

Add vinegar to milk to sour it. Let the mixture stand a few minutes before mixing. Stir dry ingredients together and mix well. In a large bowl, stir together the molasses, milk, and raisins. Add the dry ingredients in several portions, beating well after each. Butter an empty 1 lb. coffee tin and pour the batter in. Cover with buttered wax paper and aluminum foil. Arrange the cover so that it is puffed up (to allow room for expansion) yet airtight. Set the tin on a rack in a pan of water that comes 1/4 the way up the sides of the coffee tin. Cover the steamer, bring the water to a boil and simmer for 2 hours. Check the level of water once or twice. Makes 1 loaf.

Boston

APPLE-CINNAMON MUFFINS

3/4	**cup unsalted butter, softened**
1 2/3	**cups sugar**
2	**large eggs**
2	**teaspoons vanilla extract**
2 1/4	**cups flour**
1	**tablespoon ground cinnamon**
1 3/4	**teaspoons baking powder**
1	**teaspoon salt**
1 1/2	**cups milk**
1	**cup Granny Smith apples, peeled and chopped**
	Cinnamon sugar (1/2 cup sugar with 1 tablespoon cinnamon)

In mixing bowl, cream butter with sugar until fluffy. Add eggs, one at a time, beating until well combined. Add vanilla. Stir together flour, cinnamon, baking powder and salt in another bowl.

Add alternately with milk to the butter-egg mixture, stirring only to blend. Fold in apples carefully. Fill 12 paper-cup-lined muffin cups at least 2/3 full with batter. Sprinkle each muffin with 1 teaspoon cinnamon-sugar. Bake at 350 degrees 25 to 30 minutes or until tops spring back when lightly touched. Serve warm. Makes 12 large muffins.

CINNAMON ROLLS

1	**package active dry yeast**
1/4	**cup warm water**
1	**cup milk, scalded, then cooled**
3-4	**cups flour, approximately**
1/4	**cup butter**
3	**tablespoons sugar**
1	**egg, slightly beaten**
1	**teaspoon salt**
1/2	**cup raisins**

Filling:

1/4	**cup butter, softened**
1/2	**cup brown sugar**
1	**teaspoon cinnamon**

Dissolve yeast in water. Stir in cooled milk and 1 cup of flour, beating until smooth; let stand until light and bubbly, about 1/2 hour. Cream together the butter and sugar. Add egg and salt. Work in remaining flour to make a soft dough. Add raisins. Knead until smooth and elastic. Place in greased bowl, cover, and let rise in warm place until doubled, about 1 hour. Roll dough out into a rectangle 12 x 18 inches. Spread with softened butter. Sprinkle on the brown sugar and cinnamon. Roll up jelly-roll fashion. Slice into 24 pieces. Place rolls close together in buttered 9 x 13 inch baking pan. Let rise again until doubled. Bake in 375 degree preheated oven for approximately 20 minutes. Remove from pan by turning out onto a rack. While still warm, dribble icing over the rolls.

Cinnamon Rolls

Boston Cream Pie

BOSTON CREAM PIE

1/2 cup butter
1 cup sugar
2 eggs, beaten
2 cups sifted flour
$2^{1/2}$ teaspoons baking powder
1/2 teaspoon salt
1/2 cup milk
1 teaspoon vanilla

Cream filling:

3/4 cup sugar
1/3 cup flour
1/4 teaspoon salt
2 cups scalded milk
2 eggs
1 tablespoon butter
1 teaspoon vanilla

Glaze:

1/2 cup sugar
3 tablespoons light corn syrup
2 tablespoons water
4 squares (ounces) semisweet chocolate, coarsely chopped

Pie: Cream together the butter and sugar until light. Add eggs and mix well. Add the sifted dry ingredients alternately with milk. Add vanilla and bake in 2 9-inch greased layer pans lined with waxed paper in a preheated 375 degree oven about 25 minutes. When cool, remove from pans and fill with the cream filling.

Filling: Mix together the sugar, flour and salt. Over this, pour the scalded milk. Stir and cook until thickened. Mix in quickly 2 eggs, slightly beaten, and cook another 2 minutes. Remove from heat, add the butter and vanilla. Cool.

Glaze: In saucepan, bring sugar, syrup and water to a boil over low heat. Stir constantly. Remove from heat, add chocolate. Let stand a minute or two. Whisk until smooth. Pour glaze over pie and let drip down the sides.

BLUEBERRY GRUNT (SLUMP)

Developed to be cooked on an open hearth, without the necessity of using an oven, it could have been a main course or breakfast in early New England. This fruit and dumpling dish is also considered a dessert.

1$^{1/4}$	**cups water**
3/4	**cup sugar**
2	**teaspoons cornstarch**
	Juice of 1 lemon
3	**cups blueberries**

Combine water, sugar, cornstarch, and lemon juice in a large skillet. Bring to a boil, stirring to keep smooth, cover and simmer 5 minutes. Add berries and cook additional 2 minutes. Drop dumpling batter by teaspoon into the berry mixture. Cover tightly and cook on simmer for 12 minutes. Do not lift lid. Serve with dollops if whipped cream.

Dumplings:

1$^{1/2}$	**cups flour**
3$^{1/2}$	**teaspoons baking powder**
1/2	**teaspoon salt**
2	**teaspoons sugar**
1/4	**cup milk**

Sift flour 2 times with baking powder, salt and sugar. Add milk and stir with a fork until blended.

Blueberry Grunt

RAISIN PIE

1	**cup raisins**
2	**cups water**
1/2	**cup sugar**
1	**egg**
3$^{1/2}$	**tablespoons flour**
1/4	**teaspoon salt**
1	**tablespoon butter**
2	**tablespoons butter**
1	**tablespoon lemon juice**
1	**teaspoon lemon zest**
	Pastry for one 9 inch pie

Add warm water to raisins, cover and cook slowly for 20 minutes. Drain and add enough water to the juice to make 2 cups. Combine the flour, sugar, salt and the liquid. Cook over medium heat until thickened, stirring constantly. Pour small amount of hot mixture over beaten egg. Stir well. Return to saucepan and bring to a boil. Remove, add the lemon juice and zest. Cool. Pour into baked pie shell. Chill. When ready to serve cover top with whipped cream.

SUGAR COOKIES

1	**cup butter**
1	**cup confectioners sugar**
1	**cup granulated sugar**
2	**eggs**
1	**cup oil**
2	**teaspoons vanilla**
1	**teaspoon baking soda**
1	**teaspoon cream of tartar**
1/2	**teaspoon salt**
5	**cups flour**
	Granulated sugar for dipping

In medium bowl, cream butter with confectioners sugar and granulated sugar. Beat in eggs until smooth. Slowly stir in oil, vanilla, baking soda, cream of tartar, salt and flour. Chill for easy handling. Shape into walnut-size balls. Dip in sugar. Place on baking sheet and press down. Bake in preheated oven at 350 degrees for 10 -12 minutes. Makes about 4 dozen cookies.

Apple Pie

APPLE PIE

	Pastry for 2 crust pie
6	**cups tart apples like Granny Smith, peeled and sliced**
2/3	**cup sugar**
3	**tablespoons flour**
1	**teaspoon lemon juice**
1-2	**teaspoons cinnamon**
1/2	**teaspoon nutmeg**
2	**tablespoons butter**

Line a deep 9 inch pie pan with pastry. In a large bowl, mix together the sliced apples, sugar, flour, lemon juice and spices. Fill the pie shell with the mixture. Dot with butter. Cover with top crust, sealing edges well. Sprinkle with sugar and bake in a preheated 375 degree oven for approximately 50 minutes. Makes 8 servings.

Pastry:

2	**cups flour**
1	**teaspoon salt**
2/3	**cup shortening, very cold**
1/4	**cup very cold water**

In large bowl, cut shortening into dry ingredients until mixture is crumbly. Using a fork, add the water in portions until ball is formed. Chill in refrigerator for 30 minutes. Divide in half. Roll each into a 15 inch circle, about 1/8 inch thick. In top crust, make several small slashes for venting.

BLUEBERRY CAKE

2	**eggs, separated**
1	**cup sugar**
1/2	**cup solid shortening**
1/4	**teaspoon salt**
1	**teaspoon vanilla**
$1^{1/2}$	**cups flour**
$1^{1/2}$	**cups blueberries**
1	**teaspoon baking powder**
1/3	**cup milk**
	Granulated sugar

Beat egg whites with 1/4 cup sugar in medium mixing bowl until mixture forms stiff, shiny peaks. Set aside. Cream shortening in a large mixing bowl. Add salt and vanilla. Gradually add remaining 3/4 cup sugar. Add egg yolks and beat until light and creamy. Take a small amount of the flour and toss with the blueberries (so they do not go to bottom). Add remaining dry ingredients alternately with milk. Fold in the egg whites and blueberries. Pour batter into a greased 8 inch square pan. Sprinkle top of batter lightly with sugar. Bake in preheated 350 degree oven approximately 50-60 minutes.

Gingerbread

OLD-FASHIONED GINGERBREAD

1/3 cup shortening
1 cup sugar
2 eggs
1/2 cup molasses
1 cup sour cream
2 cups sifted flour
1 teaspoon baking soda
1/2 teaspoon salt
$1^{1/2}$ teaspoons ground ginger
1/4 teaspoon ground cloves

Cream shortening and sugar; add eggs, one at a time beating well after each addition. Stir in molasses and sour cream. Blend in the dry ingredients, and beat 2 minutes. Bake in greased 9 x 13 inch pan in a preheated 350 degree oven until cake tests done.

CRANBERRY DESSERT

2 cups cranberries, chopped finely
1 large banana
2/3 cup granulated sugar
2 cups crushed vanilla wafers
1/2 cup butter
1 cup confectioners sugar
2 eggs
1/2 cup chopped nuts
2 cups Cool Whip

Mix berries, banana and sugar. Set aside. Place 1/2 of crushed wafers in bottom of 8 in. square pan. Cream butter and confectioners sugar, add eggs and beat well. Spread over crumbs. Top with layer of fruit mixture. Sprinkle with nuts. Spread Cool Whip over top. Cover with remaining crushed wafers. Chill at least 4 hours or overnight. Serves 6.

PUMPKIN PIE

2 cups canned pureed pumpkin
2/3 cup sugar
1 teaspoon cinnamon
1/2 teaspoon ginger
1/2 teaspoon allspice
1/4 teaspoon salt
2 eggs
1 cup milk

Line a 9 inch pie tin with pastry. Mix together pumpkin, sugar, spices, salt and beaten egg. Add milk. Pour into pastry shell. Bake in preheated 375 degree oven for 50 - 60 minutes.

OLD-FASHIONED CIDER APPLE BUTTER

20 pounds tart apples
1 quart cider
Sugar (1/2 cup per 1 cup of fruit pulp)
1 tablespoon cinnamon
1 teaspoon cloves
$1^{1/2}$ teaspoons allspice

Wash apples, quarter and cook with water to half cover them., until very soft. Put through colander to measure the pulp. Add 1/2 as much sugar, the cider and spices. Cook in a large kettle on top of stove until thick and dark. Can also be baked in shallow pan in 250 - 300 degree oven. Stir frequently. Can be sealed in canning jars. Keep refrigerated if not sealed in canning jars.

INDIAN PUDDING

1/2	cup yellow cornmeal
4	cups milk
2	tablespoons butter, melted
1/2	cup molasses
1	teaspoon cinnamon
1/2	teaspoon ground ginger
1	teaspoon salt
2	eggs, separated
	Whipped unsweetened heavy cream

Place the cornmeal in the top of the double boiler, over boiling water, and gradually add the scalded milk. Stir constantly and continue to cook for 20 minutes. Remove from the heat and stir in the butter, molasses, spices, salt, and egg yolks. Set aside to cool slightly. In a clean bowl, beat the egg whites until stiff but not dry. Fold into the pudding mixture. Turn the batter into a greased baking dish and bake for approximately 40 minutes in preheated 350 degree oven.

POPCORN WITH MAPLE SYRUP

This is a real New England snack, with both popcorn and maple syrup being native American foods. Just drizzle maple syrup over hot buttered popcorn. Form into balls.

Maple Sugaring

MOLASSES SUGAR COOKIES

3/4	cup shortening
1	cup sugar
1/4	cup molasses
1	egg
2	cups sifted flour
2	teaspoons baking soda
1/2	teaspoon ground cloves
1/2	teaspoon ginger
1	teaspoon cinnamon
1/2	teaspoon salt
	Granulated sugar

Melt shortening in large saucepan over low heat. Remove from heat and cool. Add 1 cup sugar, molasses and egg. Beat well. Sift together the flour, soda, cloves, ginger, cinnamon and salt. Add to first mixture and mix well. Chill dough. Form into 1 inch balls. Roll in additional granulated sugar and place on a greased cookie sheets two inches apart. Bake in a preheated 375 degree oven 8-10 minutes.

FRENCH DRESSING

In blender place the following:

1	can cream of tomato soup
1 1/2	cups salad oil
1	cup vinegar
1	cup sugar
1 1/2	teaspoons paprika
1	teaspoon dry mustard
1	teaspoon salt
3	tablespoons Worcestershire sauce
2	tablespoons grated onion
1	teaspoon dried rosemary
1	teaspoon dried basil
1/2	teaspoon garlic powder

Blend well, about 1 minute. Refrigerate. Makes 1 quart.

Corn Fritters

CORN FRITTERS

1 cup corn, finely chopped
8 tablespoons flour
1/2 teaspoon baking powder
2 egg yolks, well beaten
2 egg whites, well beaten
Salt and pepper

Sift dry ingredients, add to corn, then add beaten egg yolks. Fold in beaten egg whites. Drop by spoonfuls into hot fat (375 degrees) and fry until golden brown. Serve with maple syrup. Serves 4.

COUNTRY FAIR CORN RELISH

6 cups corn, cut from cob
3 cups cabbage, chopped fine
1 cup onion, chopped finely
1 cup celery, chopped finely
1 cup green pepper, chopped finely
3 tablespoons salt
1 quart cider vinegar
1 cup water
2 cups sugar
2 tablespoons dry mustard
4 teaspoons turmeric
1/2 teaspoon white pepper
1/2 cup flour
1 12 ounce can pimiento, chopped finely

Mix raw vegetables and salt. Add 2 cups vinegar and bring to boiling point. Boil gently for 20 minutes. Mix sugar, spices and flour together. Add remaining 2 cups vinegar and stir until smooth. Cook until thickened, stirring constantly. Add to vegetables and cook slowly for 30 minutes. Add pimiento during last 5 minutes of cooking time. Pour into hot, sterilized jars and seal. Makes 5 pints.

WATERMELON PICKLES

3 pounds white rind of watermelon
5 cups sugar
2 cups cider vinegar
2 cups cold water
1 tablespoon cloves, whole
1 tablespoon allspice, whole
1 cinnamon stick, broken
1 lemon, sliced

Cut melon into 1 inch cubes. Let melon stand overnight in a brine of 2 tablespoons salt and 1 quart water. Drain, then cover with cold water and cook until tender. Drain. Make syrup of sugar, vinegar and water. Put spices in bag and add to syrup. Boil 5 minutes. Add melon rind and cook until watermelon is transparent. Makes 3 pints.